The Fifth Queen Crowned

The Fifth Queen Crowned

Ford Madox Ford

MINT EDITIONS

The Fifth Queen Crowned was first published in 1908.

This edition published by Mint Editions 2021.

ISBN 9781513290812 | E-ISBN 9781513293660

Published by Mint Editions®

MINT
EDITIONS

minteditionbooks.com

Publishing Director: Jennifer Newens
Design & Production: Rachel Lopez Metzger
Project Manager: Micaela Clark
Typesetting: Westchester Publishing Services

Contents

PART I
THE MAJOR CHORD

I

The Bishop of Rome—"

Thomas Cranmer began a hesitating speech. In the pause after the words the King himself hesitated, as if he poised between a heavy rage and a sardonic humour. He deemed, however, that the humour could the more terrify the Archbishop—and, indeed, he was so much upon the joyous side in those summer days that he had forgotten how to browbeat.

"Our holy father," he corrected the Archbishop. "Or I will say my holy father, since thou art a heretic—"

Cranmer's eyes had always the expression of a man's who looked at approaching calamity, but at the King's words his whole face, his closed lips, his brows, the lines from his round nose, all drooped suddenly downwards.

"Your Grace will have me write a letter to the—to his—to him—"

The downward lines fixed themselves, and from amongst them the panic-stricken eyes made a dumb appeal to the griffins and crowns of his dark green hangings, for they were afraid to turn to the King. Henry retained his heavy look of jocularity: he jumped at a weighty gibe—

"My Grace will have thy Grace write a letter to his Holiness."

He dropped into a heavy impassivity, rolled his eyes, fluttered his swollen fingers on the red and gilded table, and then said clearly, "My. Thy. His."

When he was in that mood he spoke with a singular distinctness that came up from his husky and ordinary joviality like something dire and terrible—like that something that upon a clear smooth day will suggest to you suddenly the cruelty that lies always hidden in the limpid sea.

"To Cæsar—egomet, I mineself—that which is Cæsar's: to him—that is to say to his Holiness, our lord of Rome—the things which are of God! But to thee, Archbishop, I know not what belongs."

He paused and then struck his hand upon the table: "Cold porridge is thy portion! Cold porridge!" he laughed; "for they say: Cold porridge to the devil! And, since thou art neither God's nor the King's, what may I call thee but the devil's self's man?"

A heavy and minatory silence seemed to descend upon him; the Archbishop's thin hands opened suddenly as if he were letting something fall to the ground. The King scowled heavily, but rather as if he were remembering past heavinesses than for any present griefs.

"Why," he said, "I am growing an old man. It is time I redded up my house."

It was as if he thought he could take his time, for his heavily pursed eyes looked down at the square tips of his fingers where they drummed on the table. He was such a weighty man that the old chair in which he sat creaked at the movement of his limbs. It was his affectation of courtesy that he would not sit in the Archbishop's own new gilded and great chair that had been brought from Lambeth on a mule's back along with the hangings. But the other furnishings of that Castle of Pontefract were as old as the days of Edward IV—even the scarlet wood of the table had upon it the arms of Edward IV's Queen Elizabeth, side by side with that King's. Henry noted it and said—

"It is time these arms were changed. See that you have here fairly painted the arms of my Queen and me—Howard and Tudor—in token that we have passed this way and sojourned in this Castle of Pontefract."

He was dallying with time as if it were a luxury to dally: he looked curiously round the room.

"Why, they have not housed you very well," he said, and, as the Archbishop shivered suddenly, he added, "there should be glass in the windows. This is a foul old kennel."

"I have made a complaint to the Earl Marshal," Cranmer said dismally, "but 'a said there was overmuch room needed above ground."

This room was indeed below ground and very old, strong, and damp. The Archbishop's own hangings covered the walls, but the windows shot upwards through the stones to the light; there was upon the ground of stone not a carpet but only rushes; being early in the year, no provision was made for firing, and the soot of the chimney back was damp, and sparkled with the track of a snail that had lived there undisturbed for many years, and neither increasing, because it had no mate, nor dying, because it was well fed by the ferns that, behind the present hangings, grew in the joints of the stones. In that low-ceiled and dark place the Archbishop was aware that above his head were fair and sunlit rooms, newly painted and hung, with the bosses on the ceilings fresh silvered or gilt, all these fair places having been given over to kinsmen of the yellow Earl Marshal from the Norfolk Queen downwards. And the temporal and material neglect angered him and filled him with a querulous bitterness that gnawed up even through his dread of a future—still shadowy—fall and ruin.

The King looked sardonically at the line of the ceiling. He had known that Norfolk, who was the Earl Marshal, had the mean mind to make him set these indignities upon the Archbishop, and loftily he considered this result as if the Archbishop were a cat mauled by his own dog whose nature it was to maul cats.

The Archbishop had been standing with one hand on the arm of his heavy chair, about to haul it back from the table to sit himself down. He had been standing thus when the King had entered with the brusque words—

"Make you ready to write a letter to Rome."

And he still stood there, the cold feet among the damp rushes, the cold hand still upon the arm of the chair, the cap pulled forward over his eyes, the long black gown hanging motionless to the boot tops that were furred around the ankles.

"I have made a plaint to the Earl Marshal," he said; "it is not fitting that a lord of the Church should be so housed."

Henry eyed him sardonically.

"Sir," he said, "I am being brought round to think that ye are only a false lord of the Church. And I am minded to think that ye are being brought round to trow even the like to mine own self."

His eyes rested, little and twinkling like a pig's, upon the opening of the Archbishop's cloak above his breastbone, and the Archbishop's right hand nervously sought that spot.

"I was always of the thought," he said, "that the prohibition of the wearing of crucifixes was against your Highness' will and the teachings of the Church."

A great crucifix of silver, the Man of Sorrows depending dolorously from its arms and backed up by a plaque of silver so that it resembled a porter's badge, depended over the black buttons of his undercoat. He had put it on upon the day when secretly he had married Henry to the papist Lady Katharine Howard. On the same day he had put on a hair shirt, and he had never since removed either the one or the other. He had known very well that this news would reach the Queen's ears, as also that he had fasted thrice weekly and had taken a Benedictine sub-prior out of chains in the tower to be his second chaplain.

"Holy Church! Holy Church!" the King muttered amusedly into the stiff hair of his chin and lips. The Archbishop was driven into one of his fits of panic-stricken boldness.

"Your Grace," he said, "if ye write a letter to Rome you will—for I see not how ye may avoid it—reverse all your acts of this last twenty years."

"Your Grace," the King mocked him, "by your setting on of chains, crucifixes, phylacteries, and by your aping of monkish ways, ye have reversed—well ye know it—all my and thy acts of a long time gone."

He cast himself back from the table into the leathern shoulder-straps of the chair.

"And if," he continued with sardonic good-humour, "my fellow and servant may reverse my acts—videlicet, the King's—wherefore shall not I—videlicet, the King—reverse what acts I will? It is to set me below my servants!"

"I am minded to redd up my house!" he repeated after a moment.

"Please it, your Grace—" the Archbishop muttered. His eyes were upon the door.

The King said, "Anan?" He could not turn his bulky head, he would not move his bulky body.

"My gentleman!" the Archbishop whispered.

The King looked at the opposite wall and cried out—

"Come in, Lascelles. I am about cleaning out some stables of mine."

The door moved noiselessly and heavily back, taking the hangings with it; as if with the furtive eyes and feathery grace of a blonde fox Cranmer's spy came round the great boards.

"Ay! I am doing some cleansing," the King said again. "Come hither and mend thy pen to write."

Against the King's huge bulk—Henry was wearing purple and black upon that day—and against the Archbishop's black and pillar-like form, Lascelles, in his scarlet, with his blonde and tender beard had an air of being quill-like. The bones of his knees through his tight and thin silken stockings showed almost as those of a skeleton; where the King had great chains of gilt and green jewels round his neck, and where the Archbishop had a heavy chain of silver, he had a thin chain of fine gold and a tiny badge of silver-gilt. He dragged one of his legs a little when he walked. That was the fashion of that day, because the King himself dragged his right leg, though the ulcer in it had been cured.

Sitting askew in his chair at the table, the King did not look at this gentleman, but moved the fingers of his outstretched hand in token that his crook of the leg was kneeling enough for him.

"Take your tablets and write," Henry said; "nay, take a great sheet of parchment and write—"

"Your Grace," he added to the Archbishop, "ye are the greatest penner of solemn sentences that I have in my realm. What I shall say roughly to Lascelles you shall ponder upon and set down nobly, at first in the vulgar tongue and then in fine Latin." He paused and added—

"Nay; ye shall write it in the vulgar tongue, and the Magister Udal shall set it into Latin. He is the best Latinist we have—better than myself, for I have no time—"

Lascelles was going between a great cabinet with iron hinges and the table. He fetched an inkhorn set into a tripod, a sandarach, and a roll of clean parchment that was tied around with a green ribbon.

Upon the gold and red of the table he stretched out the parchment as if it had been a map. He mended his pen with a little knife and kneeled down upon the rushes beside the table, his chin level with the edge. His whole mind appeared to be upon keeping the yellowish sheet straight and true upon the red and gold, and he raised his eyes neither to the Archbishop's white face nor yet to the King's red one.

Henry stroked the short hairs of his neck below the square grey beard. He was reflecting that very soon all the people in that castle, and very soon after, most of the people in that land would know what he was about to say.

"Write now," he said. "'Henry—by the grace of God—Defender of the Faith—King, Lord Paramount.'" He stirred in his chair.

"Set down all my styles and titles: 'Duke Palatine—Earl—Baron—Knight'—leave out nothing, for I will show how mighty I am." He hummed, considered, set his head on one side and then began to speak swiftly—

"Set it down thus: 'We, Henry, and the rest, being a very mighty King, such as few have been, are become a very humble man. A man broken by years, having suffered much. A man humbled to the dust, crawling to kiss the wounds of his Redeemer. A Lord of many miles both of sea and land.'" Why, say—

"'Guide and Leader of many legions, yet comes he to thee for guidance.' Say, too, 'He who was proud cometh to thee to regain his pride. He who was proud in things temporal cometh to thee that he may once more have the pride of a champion in Christendom—'"

He had been speaking as if with a malicious glee, for his words seemed to strike, each one, into the face of the pallid figure, darkly standing before him. And he was aware that each word increased the stiff and watchful constraint of the figure that knelt beside the table to write. But suddenly his glee left him; he scowled at the Archbishop as if Cranmer had caused him to sin. He pulled at the collar around his throat.

"No," he cried out, "write down in simple words that I am a very sinful man. Set it down that I grow old! That I am filled with fears for my poor soul! That I have sinned much! That I recall all that I have done! An old man, I come to my Saviour's Regent upon earth. A man aware of error, I will make restitution tenfold! Say I am broken and aged and afraid! I kneel down on the ground—"

He cast his inert mass suddenly a little forward as if indeed he were about to come on to his knees in the rushes.

"Say—" he muttered—"say—"

But his face and his eyes became suffused with blood.

"It is a very difficult thing," he uttered huskily, "to meddle in these sacred matters."

He fell heavily back into his chair-straps once more.

"I do not know what I will have you to say," he said.

He looked broodingly at the floor.

"I do not know," he muttered.

He rolled his eyes, first to the face of the Archbishop, then to Lascelles—

"Body of God—what carved turnips!" he said, for in the one face there was only panic, and in the other nothing at all. He rolled on to his feet, catching at the table to steady himself.

"Write what you will," he called, "to these intents and purposes. Or stay to write—I will send you a letter much more good from the upper rooms."

Cranmer suddenly stretched out, with a timid pitifulness, his white hands. But, rolling his huge shoulders, like a hastening bear, the King went over the rushes. He pulled the heavy door to with such a vast force that the latch came again out of the hasp, and the door, falling slowly back and quivering as if with passion, showed them his huge legs mounting the little staircase.

A LONG SILENCE FELL IN that dim room. The Archbishop's lips moved silently, the spy's glance went, level, along his parchment. Suddenly he grinned mirthlessly and as if at a shameless thought.

"The Queen will write the letter his Grace shall send us," he said.

Then their eyes met. The one glance, panic-stricken, seeing no issue, hopeless and without resource, met the other—crafty, alert, fox-like, with a dance in it. The glances transfused and mingled. Lascelles remained upon his knees as if, stretching out his right knee behind him, he were taking a long rest.

II

I t was almost within earshot of these two men in their dim cell that
the Queen walked from the sunlight into shadow and out again.
This great terrace looked to the north and west, and, from the little
hillock, dominating miles of gently rising ground, she had a great view
over rolling and very green country. The original builders of the Castle
of Pontefract had meant this terrace to be flagged with stone: but the
work had never been carried so far forward. There was only a path
of stone along the bowshot and a half of stone balustrade; the rest
had once been gravel, but the grass had grown over it; that had been
scythed, and nearly the whole space was covered with many carpets of
blue and red and other very bright colours. In the left corner when you
faced inwards there was a great pavilion of black cloth, embroidered
very closely with gold and held up by ropes of red and white. Though
forty people could sit in it round the table, it appeared very small, the
walls of the castle towered up so high. They towered up so high, so
square, and so straight that from the terrace below you could hardly
hear the flutter of the huge banner of St George, all red and white
against the blue sky, though sometimes in a gust it cracked like a huge
whip, and its shadow, where it fell upon the terrace, was sufficient to
cover four men.

To take away from the grimness of the flat walls many little banners
had been suspended from loopholes and beneath windows. Swallow-
tailed, long, or square, they hung motionless in the shelter, or, since the
dying away of the great gale three days before, had looped themselves
over their staffs. These were all painted green, because that was the
Queen's favourite colour, being the emblem of Hope.

A little pavilion, all of green silk, at the very edge of the platform,
had all its green curtains looped up, so that only the green roof showed;
and, within, two chairs, a great leathern one for the King, a little one
of red and white wood for the Queen, stood side by side as if they
conversed with each other. At the top of it was a golden image of a lion,
and above the peak of the entrance another, golden too, of the Goddess
Flora, carrying a cornucopia of flowers, to symbolise that this tent was
a summer abode for pleasantness.

Here the King and Queen, for the four days that they had been in
the castle, had delighted much to sit, resting after their long ride up

FORD MADOX FORD

from the south country. For it pleased Henry to let his eyes rest upon a great view of this realm that was his, and to think nothing; and it pleased Katharine Howard to think that now she swayed this land, and that soon she would alter its face.

They looked out, over the tops of the elm trees that grew right up against the terrace wall; but the land itself was too green, the fields too empty of dwellings. There was no one but sheep between all the hedgerows: there was, in all the wide view, but one church tower, and where, in place and place, there stood clusters of trees as if to shelter homesteads—nearly always the homesteads had fallen to ruin beneath the boughs. Upon one ridge one could see the long walls of an unroofed abbey. But, to the keenest eye no men were visible, save now and then a shepherd leaning on his crook. There was no ploughland at all. Now and then companies of men in helmets and armour rode up to or away from the castle. Once she had seen the courtyard within the keep filled with cattle that lowed uneasily. But these, she had learned, had been taken from cattle thieves by the men of the Council of the Northern Borders. They were destined for the provisioning of that castle during her stay there, they being forfeit, whether Scotch or English.

"Ah," she said, "whilst his Grace rides north to meet the King's Scots I will ride east and west and south each day."

At that moment, whilst the King had left Cranmer and his spy and, to regain his composure, was walking up and down in her chamber, she was standing beside the Duke of Norfolk about midway between the end of the terrace and the little green pavilion.

She was all in a dark purple dress, to please the King whose mood that colour suited; and the Duke's yellow face looked out above a suit all of black. He wore that to please the King too, for the King was of opinion that no gathering looked gay in its colours that had not many men in black amongst the number.

He said—

"You do not ride north with his Grace?"

He leaned upon his two staves, one long and of silver, the other shorter and gilt; his gown fell down to his ankles, his dark and half-closed eyes looked out at a tree that, struck lately by lightning, stretched up half its boughs all naked from a little hillock beside a pond a mile away.

"So it is settled between his Grace and me," she said. She did not much like her uncle, for she had little cause. But, the King being away, she walked with him rather than with another man.

"I ask, perforce," he said, "for I have much work in the ordering of your progresses."

"We meant that you should have that news this day," she said.

He shot one glance at her face, then turned his eyes again upon the stricken tree. Her face was absolutely calm and without expression, as it had been always when she had directed him what she would have done. He could trace no dejection in it: on the other hand, he gave her credit for a great command over her features. That he had himself. And, in the niece's eyes, as they moved from the backs of a flock of sheep to the dismantled abbey on the ridge, there was something of the enigmatic self-containment that was in the uncle's steady glance. He could observe no dejection, and at that he humbled himself a little more.

"Ay," he said, "the ordering of your progresses is a heavy burden. I would have you commend what I have done here."

She looked at him, at that, as if with a swift jealousy. His eyes were roving upon the gay carpets, the pavilions, and the flags against the grim walls, depending in motionless streaks of colour.

"The King's Grace's self," she said, "did tell me that all these things he ordered and thought out for my pleasuring."

Norfolk dropped his eyes to the ground.

"Aye," he said, "his Grace ordered them and their placing. There is no man to equal his Grace for such things; but I had the work of setting them where they are. I would have your favour for that."

She appeared appeased and gave him her hand to kiss. There was a little dark mole upon the third finger.

"The last niece that I had for Queen," he said, "would not suffer me to kiss her hand."

She looked at him a little absently, for, because since she had been Queen—and before—she had been a lonely woman, she was given to thinking her own thoughts whilst others talked.

She was troubled by the condition of her chief maid Margot Poins. Margot Poins was usually tranquil, modest, submissive in a cheerful manner and ready to converse. But of late she had been moody, and sunk in a dull silence. And that morning she had suddenly burst out into a smouldering, heavy passion, and had torn Katharine's hair whilst she dressed it.

"Ay," Margot had said, "you are Queen: you can do what you will. It is well to be Queen. But we who are dirt underfoot, we cannot do one single thing."

And, because she was lonely, with only Lady Rochford, who was foolish, and this girl to talk to, it had grieved the Queen to find this girl growing so lumpish and dull. At that time, whilst her hair was being dressed, she had answered only—

"Yea; it is good to be a Queen. But you will find it in Seneca—" and she had translated for Margot the passage which says that eagles are as much tied by weighty ropes as are finches caught in tiny fillets.

"Oh, your Latin," Margot had said. "I would I had never heard the sound of it, but had stuck to clean English."

Katharine imagined then that it was some new flame of the Magister Udal's that was troubling the girl, and this troubled her too, for she did not like that her maids should be played with by men, and she loved Margot for her past loyalties, readiness, and companionship.

SHE CAME OUT OF HER thoughts to say to her uncle, remembering his speech about her hands—

"Aye; I have heard that Anne Boleyn had six fingers upon her right hand."

"She had six upon each, but she concealed it," he answered. "It was her greatest grief."

Katharine realised that his sardonic tone, his bitter yellow face, the croak in his voice, and his stiff gait—all these things were signs of his hostility to her. And his mention of Anne Boleyn, who had been Queen, much as she was, and of her bitter fate, this mention, if it could not be a threat, was, at least, a reminder meant to give her fears and misgiving. When she had been a child—and afterwards, until the very day when she had been shown for Queen—her uncle had always treated her with a black disdain, as he treated all the rest of the world. When he had—and it was rarely enough—come to visit her grandmother, the old Duchess of Norfolk, he had always been like that. Through the old woman's huge, lonely, and ugly halls he had always stridden, halting a little over the rushes, and all creatures must keep out of his way. Once he had kicked her little dog, once he had pushed her aside; but probably, then, when she had been no more than a child, he had not known who she was, for she had lived with the servants and played with the servants' children, much like one of them, and her grandmother had known little of the household or its ways.

She answered him sharply—

"I have heard that you were no good friend to your niece, Anne Boleyn, when she was in her troubles."

He swallowed in his throat and gazed impassively at the distant oak tree, nevertheless his knee trembled with fury. And Katharine knew very well that if, more than another, he took pleasure in giving pain with his words, he bore the pain of other's words less well than most men.

"The Queen Anne," he said, "was a heretic. No better was she than a Protestant. She battened upon the goods of our Church. Why should I defend her?"

"Uncle," she said, "where got you the jewel in your bonnet?"

He started a little back at that, and the small veins in his yellow eye-whites grew inflamed with blood.

"Queen—" he brought out between rage and astonishment that she should dare the taunt.

"I think it came from the great chalice of the Abbey of Rising," she said. "We are valiant defenders of the Church, who wear its spoils upon our very brows."

It was as if she had thrown down a glove to him and to a great many that were behind him.

She knew very well where she stood, and she knew very well what her uncle and his friends awaited for her, for Margot, her maid, brought her alike the gossip of the Court and the loudly voiced threats and aspirations of the city. For the Protestants—she knew them and cared little for them. She did not believe there were very many in the King's and her realm, and mostly they were foreign merchants and poor men who cared little as long as their stomachs were filled. If these had their farms again they would surely return to the old faith, and she was minded to do away with the sheep. For it was the sheep that had brought discontent to England. To make way for these fleeces the ploughmen had been dispossessed.

It was natural that Protestants should hate her; but with Norfolk and his like it was different. She knew very well that Norfolk came there that day and waited every day, watching anxiously for the first sign that the King's love for her should cool. She knew very well that they said in the Court that with the King it was only possession and then satiety. And she knew very well that when Norfolk's eyes searched her face it was for signs of dismay and of discouragement. And when Norfolk had said that he himself had placed the banners, the tents, the pavilions and carpets that made gay all that grim terrace of the air, he was essaying to make her think that the King was abandoning the task of doing her honour. This had made her angry, for it was such folly. Her uncle should have known that the King had discussed all these things with her, asking her what she liked, and that all these bright colours and these plaisaunces were what her man had gallantly thought out for her. She carried her challenge still further.

"It ill becomes us Howards and all like us," she said, "to talk of how we will defend the Church of God—"

"I am a swordsman only," he said. "Give me that—"

She was not minded to listen to him.

"It becomes us ill," she said; "and I take shame in it. For, a very few years agone we Howards were very poor. Now we are very rich—though it is true that my father is still a very poor man, and your stepmother, my grandmother, has known hard shifts. But we Howards, through you who are our head, became amongst the richest in the land. And how?"

"I have done services—" the Duke began.

"Why, there has been no new wealth made in this realm," she said; "it came from the Church. Consider what you have had of this Abbey of Risings that I speak of, because I knew it well as a child, and saw many times then, sparkling in that which held the blood of my Saviour, the jewel that is now in your cap."

The Abbey of Risings, after the visitors had been to it and the monks had been driven out, had fallen to the Duke of Norfolk. And his men had stripped the lead from the roofs, the glass from the windows, the very tiles from the floor. And this little abbey was only one of many, large and small, that had fallen to the Duke, so that it was true enough that, through him, the Howards had become a very rich family.

Norfolk burst into a sudden speech—

"I hold these things only as a trust," he said. "I am ready to restore."

"Why, that is very well," Katharine said; "and I have hopes that soon you will be called to make that restoration to your God."

Norfolk looked at the square toes of his shoes for a long time.

"Will you have *all* things to be given back?" he said at last after he had thought much.

"The King will have all things be as they were before the Queen Katharine, my namesake of Aragon, was undone," Katharine answered. "And me he will have to take her place so that all things shall be as before they were."

The Duke, leaning on his silver and gold staves, shrugged his shoulders very slowly.

"This will make a very great confusion," he said.

"Ay," Katharine answered, "there will a very many be confounded, and a great number of hundreds be much annoyed."

She broke in again upon his slow meditations—

"Sir," she said, "this is a very pitiful thing! Privy Seal that is dead and done with worked with a very great cunning. Well he knew that for most men the heart resideth in the pocket. Therefore, though ye said all that he rode this land with a bridle of iron, he was very careful to stop all your mouths alike with pieces of gold. It was not only to his friends that he gave what had been taken from God, but he was very careful that much also should fall into the greedy mouths of those that cried out. If he had not done this, do you think that he would have remained so long above the earth that he made weary? No. But since he made all rich alike with this plunder, so there was no man, either Catholic or Lutheran, very anxious to have him away. And, now that he is dead he worketh still. For who among you lords that do call yourselves sons of the Church, but holdeth of the Church's goods? Oh, bethink you! bethink you! The moment is at hand when ye may work restoration. See that ye do it willingly and with good hearts, smoothing and making plain the way by which the bruised feet of our Saviour shall come across this, His land."

Norfolk kept his eyes upon the ground.

"Why, for me," he said, "I am very willing. This day I will send to set clerks at work discovering that which is mine and that which came from the Church; but I think you will find some that will not do it so eagerly."

She believed him very little; and she said—

"Why, if you will do this thing I think there will not many be behindhand."

He did what he could to conceal his wincing, and her voice changed its tone.

"Sir," she said, and she was eager and pleading, "you have many men that take counsel with you, for I trow that you and my Lord of

Winchester do lead such lords as be Catholic in this realm. I know very well that you and my Lord Bishop of Winchester and such Catholic lords would have me to be your puppet and so work as you would have me, giving back to the Church such things as have fallen to Protestants or to men that ye mislike. But that may not be, for, since I owe mine advancement not to you, nor to mine own efforts, but to God alone, so to God alone do I owe fealty."

She stretched out towards him the hand that he had kissed. The tail of her coif fell almost to her feet; her body in the fresh sunlight was all cased in purple velvet, only the lawn of her undershirt showed, white and tremulous at her wrists and her neck; and, fair and contrasted with the gold of her hair, her face came out of its abstraction, to take on a pitiful and mournful earnestness.

"Sir," she said, "if you shall speak for God in the councils that you will hold, believe that your rewards shall be very great. I think that you have been a man of a very troubled mind, for you have thought only or mostly of the affairs of this world. But do now this one good stroke for God His piteous sake, and such a peace shall descend upon you as you have never yet known. You shall have no more griefs; you shall have no more fears. And that is better than the jewels of chalices, and than much lead from the roofs of abbeys. Speak you thus in these councils that you shall hold, give you such advice to them that come to you seeking it, and this I promise you—for it is too little a thing to promise you the love of a Queen and a King's favour, though that too ye shall not lack—but this I promise you, that there shall descend upon your heart that most blessed miracle and precious wealth, the peace of God."

III

When Henry was calmed by his pacing in her chamber he came out to her in the sunlight, rolling and bear-like, and so huge that the terrace seemed to grow smaller.

"Chuck," he said to her, "I ha' done a thing to pleasure thee." He moved two fingers upwards to save the Duke of Norfolk from falling to his knees, caught Katharine by the elbow, and, turning upon himself as on a huge pivot, swung her round him so that they faced the pavilion. "Sha't not talk with a citron-faced uncle," he said; "sha't save sweet words for me. I will tell thee what I ha' done to pleasure thee."

"Save it a while and do another ere ye tell me," she said.

"Now, what is your reasoning about that, wise one?" he asked.

She laughed at him, for she took pleasure in his society and, except when she was earnest to beg things of him, she was mostly gay at his side.

"It takes a woman to teach kings," she said.

He answered that it took a Queen to teach him.

"Why," she said, "listen! I know that each day ye do things to pleasure me, things prodigal or such little things as giving me pouncet boxes. But you will find—and a woman, quean or queen, knows it well—that to take the full pleasure of her lover's surprises well, she must have an easy mind. And to have an easy mind she must have granted her the little, little boons she asketh."

He reflected ponderously upon this point and at last, with a sort of peasant's gravity, nodded his head.

"For," she said, "if a woman is to take pleasure she must guess at what you men have done for her. And if she be to guess pleasurably, she must have a clear mind. And if I am to have a clear mind I must have a maiden consoled with a husband."

Henry seated himself carefully in the great chair of the small pavilion. He spread out his knees, blinked at the view and when, having cast a look round to see that Norfolk was gone—for it did not suit her that he should see on what terms she was with the King—she seated herself on a little foot-pillow at his feet, he set a great hand upon her head. She leaned her arms across over his knees, and looked up at him appealingly.

"I do take it," he said, "that I must make some man rich to wed some poor maid."

"Oh, Solomon!" she said.

"And I do take it," he continued with gravity, "that this maid is thy maid Margot."

"How know you that?" she said.

"I have observed her," he maintained gravely.

"Why, you could not well miss her," she answered. "She is as big as a plough-ox."

"I have observed," he said—and he blinked his little eyes as if, pleasurably, she were, with her words, whispering around his head. "I have observed that ye affected her."

"Why, she likes me well. She is a good wench—and today she tore my hair."

"Then that is along of a man?" he asked. "Didst not stick thy needle in her arm? Or wilto be quit of her?"

She rubbed her chin.

"Why, if she wed, I mun be quit of her," she said, as if she had never thought of that thing.

He answered—

"Assuredly; for ye may not part man and lawful wife were you seven times Queen."

"Why," she said, "I have little pleasure in Margot as she is."

"Then let her go," he answered.

"But I am a very lonely Queen," she said, "for you are much absent."

He reflected pleasurably.

"Thee wouldst have about thee a little company of well-wishers?"

"So that they be those thou lovest well," she said.

"Why, thy maid contents me," he answered. He reflected slowly. "We must give her man a post about thee," he uttered triumphantly.

"Why, trust thee to pleasure me," she said. "You will find out a way always."

He scrubbed her nose gently with his heavy finger.

"Who is the man?" he said. "What ruffler?"

"I think it is the Magister Udal," she answered.

Henry said—

"Oh ho! oh ho!" And after a moment he slapped his thigh and laughed like a child. She laughed with him, silvery upon a little sound between "ah" and "e." He stopped his laugh to listen to hers, and then he said gravely—

"I think your laugh is the prettiest sound I ever heard. I would give thy maid Margot a score of husbands to make thee laugh."

"One is enough to make her weep," she said; "and I may laugh at thee."

He said—

"Let us finish this business within the hour. Sit you upon your chair that I may call one to send this ruffler here."

She rose, with one sinuous motion that pleased him well, half to her feet and, feeling behind her with one hand for the chair, aided herself with the other upon his shoulder because she knew that it gave him joy to be her prop.

"Call the maid, too," she said, "for I would come to the secret soon."

That pleased him too, and, having shouted for a knave he once more shook with laughter.

"Oh ho," he said, "you will net this old fox, will you?"

And, having sent his messenger off to summon the Magister from the Lady Mary's room, and the maid from the Queen's, he continued for a while to soliloquise as to Udal's predicament. For he had heard the Magister rail against matrimony in Latin hexameters and doggerel Greek. He knew that the Magister was an incorrigible fumbler after petticoats. And now, he said, this old fox was to be bagged and tied up.

He said—

"Well, well, well; well, well!"

For, if a Queen commanded a marriage, a marriage there must be; there was no more hope for the Magister than for any slave of Cato's. He was cabined, ginned, trapped, shut in from the herd of bachelors. It pleased the King very well.

The King grasped the gilded arms of his great chair, Katharine sat beside him, her hands laid one within another upon her lap. She did not say one single word during the King's interview with Magister Udal.

The Magister fell upon his knees before them and, seeing the laughing wrinkles round the King's little eyes, made sure that he was sent for—as had often been the case—to turn into Latin some jest the King had made. His gown fell about his kneeling shins, his cap was at his side, his lean, brown, and sly face, with the long nose and crafty eyes, was like a woodpecker's.

"Goodman Magister," Henry said. "Stand up. We have sent for thee to advance thee." Without moving his head he rolled his eyes to one side. He loved his dramatic effects and wished to await the coming of the Queen's maid, Margot, before he gave the weight of his message.

Udal picked up his cap and came up to his feet before them; he had beneath his gown a little book, and one long finger between its leaves to keep his place where he had been reading. For he had forgotten a saying of Thales, and was reading through Cæsar's Commentaries to find it.

"As Seneca said," he uttered in his throat, "advancement is doubly sweet to them that deserve it not."

"Why," the King said, "we advance thee on the deserts of one that finds thee sweet, and is sweet to one doubly sweet to us, Henry of Windsor that speak sweet words to thee."

The lines on Udal's face drooped all a little downwards.

"Y'are reader in Latin to the Lady Mary," the King said.

"I have little deserved in that office," Udal answered; "the lady reads Latin better than even I."

"Why, you lie in that," Henry said, "'a readeth well for she's my daughter; but not so well as thee."

Udal ducked his head; he was not minded to carry modesty further than in reason.

"The Lady Mary—the Lady Mary of England—" the King said weightily—and these last two words of his had a weight all their own, so that he added, "of England" again, and then, "will have little longer need of thee. She shall wed with a puissant Prince."

"I hail, I felicitate, I bless the day I hear those words," the Magister said.

"Therefore," the King said—and his ears had caught the rustle of Margot's grey gown—"we will let thee no more be reader to that my daughter."

Margot came round the green silk curtains that were looped on the corner posts of the pavilion. When she saw the Magister her great, fair face became slowly of a fiery red; slowly and silently she fell, with motions as if bovine, to her knees at the Queen's side. Her gown was all grey, but it had roses of red and white silk round the upper edges of the square neck-place, and white lawn showed beneath her grey cap.

"We advance thee," Henry said, "to be Chancellier de la Royne, with an hundred pounds by the year from my purse. Do homage for thine office."

Udal fell upon one knee before Katharine, and dropping both cap and book, took her hand to raise to his lips. But Margot caught her hand when he had done with it and set upon it a huge pressure.

"But, Sir Chancellor," the King said, "it is evident that so grave an office must have a grave fulfiller. And, to ballast thee the better, the Queen of her graciousness hath found thee a weighty helpmeet. So that, before you shall touch the duties and emoluments of this charge you shall, and that even tonight, wed this Madam Margot that here kneels."

Udal's face had been of a coppery green pallor ever since he had heard the title of Chancellor.

"Eheu!" he said, "this is the torture of Tantalus that might never drink."

In its turn the face of Margot Poins grew pale, pushed forward towards him; but her eyes appeared to blaze, for all they were a mild blue, and the Queen felt the pressure upon her hand grow so hard that it pained her.

The King uttered the one word, "Magister!"

Udal's fingers picked at the fur of his moth-eaten gown.

"God be favourable to me," he said. "If it were anything but Chancellor!"

The King grew more rigid.

"Body of God," he said, "will you wed with this maid?"

"Ahí!" the Magister wailed; and his perturbation had in it something comic and scarecrowlike, as if a wind shook him from within. "If you will make me anything but a Chancellor, I will. But a Chancellor, I dare not."

The King cast himself back in his chair. The suggested gibe rose furiously to his lips; the Magister quailed and bent before him, throwing out his hands.

"Sire," he said, "if—which God forbid—this were a Protestant realm I might do it. But oh, pardon and give ear. Pardon and give ear—"

He waved one hand furiously at the silken canopy above them.

"It is agreed with one of mine in Paris that she shall come hither— God forgive me, I must make avowal, though God knows I would not—she shall come hither to me if she do hear that I have risen to be a Chancellor."

The King said, "Body of God!" as if it were an earthquake.

"If it were anything else but Chancellor she might not come, and I would wed Margot Poins more willingly than any other. But—God knows I do not willingly make this avowal, but am in a corner, *sicut vulpis in lucubris*, like a fox in the coils—this Paris woman is my wife."

Henry gave a great shout of laughter, but slowly Margot Poins fell across the Queen's knees. She uttered no sound, but lay there motionless. The sight affected Udal to an epileptic fury.

"Jove be propitious to me!" he stuttered out. "I know not what I can do." He began to tear the fur of his cloak and toss it over the battlements. "The woman is my wife—wed by a friar. If this were a Protestant realm now—or if I pleaded pre-contract—and God knows I ha' promised marriage to twenty women before I, in an evil day, married one—eheu!—to this one—"

He began to sob and to wring his thin hands.

"*Quod faciam? Me miser! Utinam. Utinam—*"

He recovered a little coherence.

"If this were a Protestant land ye might say this wedding was no wedding, for that a friar did it; but I know ye will not suffer that—" His eyes appealed piteously to the Queen.

"Why, then," he said, "it is not upon my head that I do not wed this wench. You be my witness that I would wed; it gores my heart to see her look so pale. It tears my vitals to see any woman look pale. As Lucretius says, 'Better the sunshine of smiles—'"

A little outputting of impatient breath from Katharine made him stop.

"It is you, your Grace," he said, "that make me thus tied. If you would let us be Protestant, or, again, if I could plead pre-contract to void this Paris marriage it would let me wed with this wench—eheu—eheu. Her brother will break my bones—"

He began to cry out so lamentably, invoking Pluto to bear him to the underworld, that the King roared out upon him—

"Why, get you gone, fool."

The Magister threw himself suddenly upon his knees, his hands clasped, his gown drooping over them down to his wrists. He turned his face to the Queen.

"Before God," he said, "before high and omnipotent Jove, I swear that when I made this marriage I thought it was no marriage!" He reflected for a breath and added, at the recollection of the cook's spits that had been turned against him when he had by woman's guile been forced into marriage with the widow in Paris, "I was driven into it by force, with sharp points at my throat. Is that not enow to void a marriage? Is that not enow? Is that not enow?"

Katharine looked out over the great levels of the view. Her face was rigid, and she swallowed in her throat, her eye being glazed and hard. The King took his cue from a glance at her face.

"Get you gone, Goodman Rogue Magister," he said, and he adopted a canonical tone that went heavily with his rustic pose. "A marriage made and consummated and properly blessed by holy friar there is no undoing. You are learned enough to know that. Rogue that you be, I am very glad that you are trapped by this marriage. Well I know that you have dangled too much with petticoats, to the great scandal of this my Court. Now you have lost your preferment, and I am glad of it. Another and a better than thou shall be the Queen's Chancellor, for another and a better than thou shall wed this wench. We will get her such a goodly husband—"

A low, melancholy wail from Margot Poins' agonised face—a sound such as might have been made by an ox in pain—brought him to a stop. It wrung the Magister, who could not bear to see a woman pained, up to a pitch of ecstatic courage.

"*Quid fecit Cæsar*," he stuttered; "what Cæsar hath done, Cæsar can do again. It was not till very lately since this canon of wedding and consummating and blessing by a holy friar hath been derided and contemned in this realm. And so it might be again—"

Katharine Howard cried out, "Ah!" Her features grew rigid and as ashen as cold steel. And, at her cry, the King—who could less bear than Udal to hear a woman in pain—the King sprang up from his chair. It was as amazing to all them as to hunters it is to see a great wild bull charge with a monstrous velocity. Udal was rigid with fear, and the King had him by the throat. He shook him backwards and forwards so that his book fell upon the Queen's feet, bursting out of his ragged gown, and his cap, flying from his opened hand, fell down over the battlement into an elm top. The King guttered out unintelligible sounds of fury from his vast chest and, planted on his huge feet, he swung the Magister round him till, backwards and staggering, the eyes growing fixed in his brown and rigid face, he was pushed, jerking at each step of the King, out of sight behind the green silk curtains.

The Queen sat motionless in her purple velvet. She twisted one hand into the chain of the medallion about her throat, and one hand lay open and pale by her side. Margot Poins knelt at her side, her face hidden in the Queen's lap, her two arms stretched out beyond her grey coifed head. For a minute she was silent. Then great sobs shook her so that Katharine swayed upon her seat. From her hidden face there came muffled and indistinguishable words, and at last Katharine said dully—

"What, child? What, child?"

Margot moved her face sideways so that her mouth was towards Katharine.

"You can unmake it! You can unmake the marriage," she brought out in huge sobs.

Katharine said—

"No! No!"

"You unmade a King's marriage," Margot wailed.

Katharine said—

"No! No!" She started and uttered the words loudly; she added pitifully, "You do not understand! You do not understand!"

It was the more pitiful in that Margot understood very well. She hid her face again and only sobbed heavily and at long intervals, and then with many sobs at once. The Queen laid her white hand upon the girl's head. Her other still played with the chain.

"Christ be piteous to me," she said. "I think it had been better if I had never married the King."

Margot uttered an indistinguishable sound.

"I think it had been better," the Queen said; "though I had jeoparded my immortal part."

Margot moved her head up to cry out in her turn—

"No! No! You may not say it!"

Then she dropped her face again. When she heard the King coming back and breathing heavily, she stood up, and with huge tears on her red and crumpled face she looked out upon the fields as if she had never seen them before. An immense sob shook her. The King stamped his foot with rage, and then, because he was soft-hearted to them that he saw in sorrow, he put his hand upon her shoulder.

"Sha't have a better mate," he uttered. "Sha't be a knight's dame! There! there!" and he fondled her great back with his hand. Her eyes screwed tightly up, she opened her mouth wide, but no words came out, and suddenly she shook her head as if she had been an enraged child. Her loud cries, shaken out of her with her tears, died away as she went across the terrace, a loud one and then a little echo, a loud one and then two more.

"Before God!" the King said, "that knave shall eat ten years of prison bread."

His wife looked still over the wooded enclosures, the little stone walls, and the copses. A small cloud had come before the sun, and its shadow was moving leisurely across the ridge where stood the roofless abbey.

"The maid shall have the best man I can give her," the King said.

"Why, no good man would wed her!" Katharine answered dully.

Henry said—

"Anan?" Then he fingered the dagger on the chain before his chest.

"Why," he added slowly, "then the Magister shall die by the rope. It is an offence that can be quitted with death. It is time such a thing were done."

Katharine's dull silence spurred him; he shrugged his shoulders and heaved a deep breath out.

"Why," he said, "a man can be found to wed the wench."

She moved one hand and uttered—

"I would not wed her to such a man!" as if it were a matter that was not much in her thoughts.

"Then she may go into a nunnery," the King said; "for before three months are out we will have many nunneries in this realm."

She looked upon him a little absently, but she smiled at him to give him pleasure. She was thinking that she wished she had not wedded him; but she smiled because, things being as they were, she thought that she had all the authorities of the noble Greeks and Romans to bid her do what a good wife should.

He laughed at her griefs, thinking that they were all about Margot Poins. He uttered jolly grossnesses; he said that she little knew the way of courts if she thought that a man, and a very good man, might not be found to wed the wench.

She was troubled that he could not better read what was upon her mind, for she was thinking that her having consented to his making null his marriage with the Princess of Cleves that he might wed her would render her work always the more difficult. It would render her more the target for evil tongues, it would set a sterner and a more stubborn opposition against her task of restoring the Kingdom of God within that realm.

Henry said—

"Ye hannot guessed what my secret was? What have I done for thee this day?"

She still looked away over the lands. She made her face smile—

"Nay, I know not. Ha' ye brought me the musk I love well?"

He shook his head.

"It is more than that!" he said.

She still smiled—

"Ha' ye—ha' ye—made make for me a new crown?"

She feared a little that that was what he had done. For he had been urgent with her, many months, to be crowned. It was his way to love these things. And her heart was a little gladder when he shook his head once again and uttered—

"It is more than that!"

She dreaded his having made ready in secret a great pageant in her honour, for she was afraid of all aggrandisements, and thought still it had been better that she had remained his sweet friend ever and not the Queen. For in that way she would have had as much empire over him, and there would have been much less clamour against her—much less clamour against the Church of her Saviour.

She forced her mind to run upon all the things that she could wish for. When she said it must be that he had ordered for her enough French taffetas to make twelve gowns, he laughed and said that he had said that it was more than a crown. When she guessed that he had made ready such a huge cavalcade that she might with great comfort and safety ride with him into Scotland, he laughed, contented that she should think of going with him upon that long journey. He stood looking at her, his little eyes blinking, his face full of pride and joy, and suddenly he uttered—

"The Church of God is come back again." He touched his cap at the sacred name. "I ha' made submission to the Pope."

He looked her full in the face to get all the delight he might from her looks and her movements.

Her blue eyes grew large; she leaned forward in her chair; her mouth opened a little; her sleeves fell down to the ground. "Now am I indeed crowned!" she said, and closed her eyes. "*Benedicta sit mater dei!*" she uttered, and her hand went over her heart place; "*deo clamavi nocte atque dië.*"

She was silent again, and she leaned more forward.

"*Sit benedicta dies haec; sit benedicta hora haec benedictaque, saeculum saeculûm, castra haec.*"

She looked out upon the great view: she aspired the air.

"*Ad colles,*" she breathed, "*levavi oculos meos; unde venit salvatio nostra!*"

"Body of God," Henry said, "all things grow plain. All things grow plain. This is the best day that ever I knew."

IV

The Lady Mary of England sat alone in a fair room with little arched windows that gave high up on to the terrace. It was the best room that ever she had had since her mother, the Queen Katharine of Aragon, had been divorced.

Dressed in black she sat writing at a large table before one window. Her paper was fitted on to a wooden pulpit that rose before her; one book stood open upon it, three others lay open too upon the red and blue and green pattern of the Saracen rug that covered her table. At her right hand was a three-tiered inkstand of pewter, set about with the white feathers of pens; and the snakelike pattern of the table-rug serpentined in and out beneath seals of parcel gilt, a platter of bread, a sandarach of pewter, books bound in wooden covers and locked with chains, books in red velvet covers, sewn with silver wire and tied with ribbons. It ran beneath a huge globe of the world, blue and pink, that had a golden pin in it to mark the city of Rome. There were little wooden racks stuck full with written papers and parchments along the wainscoting between the arched windows, but all the hangings of the other walls were of tinted and dyed silks, not any with dark colours, because Katharine Howard had deemed that that room with its deep windows in the thick walls would be otherwise dark. The room was ten paces deep by twenty long, and the wood of the floor was polished. Against the wall, behind the Lady Mary's back, there stood a high chair upon a platform. Upon the platform a carpet began that ran up the wall and, overhead, depended from the gilded rafters of the ceiling so that it formed a dais and a canopy.

The Lady Mary sat grimly amongst all these things as if none of them belonged to her. She looked in her book, she made a note upon her paper, she stretched out her hand and took a piece of bread, putting it in her mouth, swallowing it quickly, writing again, and then once more eating, for the great and ceaseless hunger that afflicted her gnawed always at her vitals.

A little boy with a fair poll was reaching on tiptoe to smell at a pink that depended from a vase of very thin glass standing in the deep window. The shield of the coloured pane cast a little patch of red and purple on to his callow head. He was dressed all in purple, very square, and with little chains and medallions, and a little dagger with a golden sheath was about his neck. In one hand he had a piece of paper, in the other a pencil. The Lady Mary wrote; the child moved on tiptoe, with a sedulous expression of silence about his lips, near to her elbow. He watched her writing for a long time with attentive eyes.

Once he said, "Sister, I—" but she paid him no heed.

After a time she looked coldly at his face and then he moved along the table, fingered the globe very gently, touched the books and returned to her side. He stood with his little legs wide apart. Then he sighed, then he said—

"Sister, the Queen did bid me ask you a question."

She looked round upon him.

"This was the Queen's question," he said bravely: "'*Cur*—why—*nunquam*—never—*rides*—dost thou smile—*cum*—when—*ego, frater tuus*—I, thy little brother—*ludo*—play—*in camerâ tuâ*—in thy chamber?'"

"Little Prince," she said, "art not afeared of me?"

"Aye, am I," he answered.

"Say then to the Queen," she said, "'*Domina Maria*—the Lady Mary—*ridet nunquam*—smileth never—*quod*—because—*timoris ratio*—the reason of my fear—*bona et satis*—is good and sufficient.'"

He held his little head upon one side.

"The Queen did bid me say," he uttered with his brave little voice, "'Holy Writ hath it: *Ecce quam bonum et dignum est fratres—fratres—*'" He faltered without embarrassment and added, "I ha' forgot the words."

"Aye!" she said, "they ha' been long forgotten in these places; I deem it is overlate to call them to mind."

She looked upon him coldly for a long time. Then she stretched out her hand for his paper.

"Your Highness, I will set you a copy."

She took his paper and wrote—

"*Malo malo malâ.*"

He held it in his chubby fist, his head on one side.

"I cannot conster it," he said.

"Why, think upon it," she answered. "When I was thy age I knew it already two years. But I was better beaten than thou."

He rubbed his little arm.

"I am beaten enow," he said.

"Knowest not what a swingeing is," she answered.

"Then thou hadst a bitter childhood," he brought out.

"I had a good mother," she cut him short.

She turned her face to her writing again; it was bitter and set. The little prince climbed slowly into the chair on the dais. He moved sturdily and curled himself up on the cushion, studying the words on the paper all the while with a little frown upon his brows. Then, shrugging his shoulders, he set the paper upon his knee and began to write.

At that date the Lady Mary was still called a bastard, though most men thought that that hardship would soon be reversed. It was said that great honours had been shown her, and that was apparent in the furnishing of her rooms, the fineness of her gear, the increase in the number of the women that waited on her, and the store of sweet things that was provided for her to eat. A great many men noted the chair with a dais that was set up always where she might be, in her principal room, and though her ladies said that she never sat in it, most men believed that she had made a pact with the King to do him honour and so to be reinstated in the estate in which she held her own. It was considered, too, that she no longer plotted with the King's enemies inside or out of the realm; it was at least certain that she no longer had men set to spy upon her, though it was noted that the Archbishop's gentleman, Lascelles, nosed about her quarters and her maids. But he was always spying somewhere and, as the Archbishop's days were thought to be numbered, he was accounted of little weight. Indeed, since the fall of Thomas Cromwell there seemed to be few spies about the Court, or almost none at all. It was known that gentlemen wrote accounts of what passed to Gardiner, the Bishop of Winchester. But Gardiner was gone back into his see and appeared to have little favour, though it was claimed for him that he had done much to advance the new Queen. So that, upon the whole, men breathed much more freely—and women too—than in the days before the fall of Privy Seal. The Queen had made little change, and seemed to have it in mind to make little more. Her relatives had, nearly none of them, been advanced. There were few Protestants oppressed, though many Catholics had been loosed from the gaols, most notably him whom the Archbishop Cranmer had taken to be his chaplain and confessor, and others that other lords had taken out of prison to be about them.

All in all the months that had passed since Cromwell's fall had gone quietly. The King and Queen had gone very often to mass since Katharine had been shown for Queen in the gardens at Hampton Court, and saints' days and the feasts of the life of our Lady had been very carefully observed, along with fasts such as had used to be observed.

The King, however, was mightily fond with his new Queen, and those that knew her well, or knew her servants well, expected great changes. Some were much encouraged, some feared very much, but nearly all were heartily glad of that summer of breathing space; and the weather was mostly good, so that the corn ripened well and there was little plague or ague abroad.

Thus most men had been heartily glad to see the new Queen upon her journey there to the north parts. She had ridden upon a white horse with the King at her side; she had asked the names of several that had come to see her; she had been fair to look at; and the King had pardoned many felons, so that men's wives and mothers had been made glad; and most old men said that the good times were come again, with the price of malt fallen and twenty-six to the score of herrings. It was reported, too, that a cider press in Herefordshire had let down a dozen firkins of cider without any apples being set in it, and this was accounted an omen of great plenty, whilst many sheep had died, so that men who had set their fields down in grass talked of giving them to the plough again, and upon St Swithin's Day no rain had fallen. All these things gave a great contentment, and many that in the hard days had thought to become Lutheran in search of betterment, now looked in byres and hidden valleys to find priests of the old faith. For if a man could plough he might eat, and if he might eat he could praise God after his father's manner as well as in a new way.

Thus, around the Lady Mary, whilst she wrote, the people of the land breathed more peace. And even she could not but be conscious of a new softness, if it was only in the warmth that came from having her window-leads properly mended. She had hardly ever before known what it was to have warm hands when she wrote, and in most days of the year she had worn fur next her skin, indoors as well as out. But now the sun beat on her new windows, and in that warmth she could wear fine lawn, so that, in spite of herself, she took pleasure and was softened, though, since she spoke to no man save the Magister Udal, and to him only about the works of Plautus or the game of cards that they played together, few knew of any change in her.

Nevertheless, on that day she had one of her more ill moods and, presently, having written a little more, she rang a small silver bell that was shaped like a Dutch woman with wide skirts.

"The Prince annoys me," she said to her woman; "send for his lady governess."

The woman, dressed all in black, like her mistress, and with a little frill of white cambric over her temples as if she were a nun, stood in the open doorway that was just level with the Lady Mary's chair, so that the stone wall of the passage caught the light from the window. She folded her hands before her.

"Alack, Madam," she said, "your Madamship knows that at this hour his Highness' lady governess taketh ever the air."

The little boy in the chair looked over his paper at his sister.

"Send for his physician then," Mary said.

"Alack, sister," the little Prince said before the woman could move, "my physician is ill. *Jacet*—He lieth—*in cubiculo*—in his bed."

The Lady Mary would not look round on him.

"Get thee, then," she uttered coldly, "to thine own apartments, Prince."

"Alack, sister," he answered, "thou knowest that I may not walk along the corridors alone for fear some slay me. Nor yet may I be anywhere save with the Queen, or thee, or with my uncles, or my lady governess, or my physicians, for fear some poison me."

He spoke with a clear and shrill voice, and the woman cast down her eyes, trembling a little, partly to hear such a small, weary child speak such a long speech as if by wizardry—for it was reported among the serving maids that he had been overlooked—and partly for fear of the black humour that she perceived to be upon her mistress.

"Send me then my Magister to lay out cards with me," the Lady Mary said. "I cannot make my studies with this Prince in my rooms."

"Alack, Madam," the girl said. She was high coloured and with dark eyes, but when she faltered then the colour died from her cheeks. The Lady Mary surveyed her coldly, for she was in the mood to give pain. She uttered no words.

"Alack, alack—" the maid whimpered. She was full of fear lest the Lady Mary should order her to receive short rations or many stripes; she was filled with consternation and grief since her sweetheart, a server, had told her that he must leave her. For it was rumoured that the Magister had been cast into gaol for sweethearting, and that the King had said that all sweethearts should be gaoled from thenceforth. "The Magister is gaoled," she said.

"Wherefore?" the Lady uttered the one expressionless word.

"I do not know," the maid wailed; "I do not know."

The form of the Archbishop's gentleman glided noiselessly behind her back. His eyes shot one sharp, sideways glance in at the door, and, like a russet fox, he was gone. He was so like a fox that the Lady Mary, when she spoke, used the words—

"Catch me that gentleman."

He was brought to the doorsill by the panting maid, for he had walked away very fast. He stood there, blinking his eyes and stroking his fox-coloured beard. When the Lady Mary beckoned him into the room he pulled off his cap and fell to his thin knees. He expected her to bid him rise, but she left him there.

"Wherefore is my secretary gaoled?" she asked cruelly.

He ran his finger round the rim of his cap where it lay on the floor beside him.

"That he is gaoled, I know," he said; "but the wherefore of it, not."

He looked down at the floor and she down at his drooped eyelids.

"God help you," she uttered scornfully. "You are a spy and yet know no more than a Queen's daughter."

"God help me," he repeated gravely and touched his eyelid with one finger. "What passed, passed between the King and him. I know no more than common report."

"Common report?" she said. "I warrant thee thou wast slinking around the terrace. I warrant thee thou heardst words of the King's mouth. I warrant thee thou followedst here to hear at my doorhole how I might take this adventure."

One of his eyelids moved delicately, but he said no word. The Lady Mary turned her back on him and he expected her order to be gone. But she turned again—

"Common report?" she uttered once more. "I do bid you give me the common report upon this, that the Queen sends to me every day this little Prince to be alone with me two hours."

He winced with his eyebrows again.

"Out with the common report," she said.

"Madam," he uttered, "it is usually commended that the Queen should seek to bring sister and Prince-brother together."

She shrugged her stiff shoulders up to her ears.

"What a poor liar for a spy," she said. "It is more usually reported"— and she turned upon the little Prince—"that the Queen sends thee here that I may work thee a mischief so that thou die and her child reign after the King thy father."

The little Prince looked at her with pensive eyes. At that moment Katharine Howard came to the room door and looked in.

"Body of God," the Lady Mary said; "here you spy out a spy committing treason. For it is still treason to kneel to me. I am of illegal birth and not of the blood royal."

Katharine essayed her smile upon the black-avised girl.

"Give me leave," she said.

"Your Grace's poor room," Mary said, "is open ever to your Grace's entry. *Ubi venis ibi tibi.*"

The Queen bade her waiting women go. She entered the room and looked at Lascelles.

"I think I know thy face," she said.

"I am the Archbishop's poor gentleman," he answered. "I think you have seen me."

"No. It is not that," she said. "It was long ago."

She crossed the room to smell at the pinks in the window.

"How late the flowers grow," she said. "It is August, yet here are still vernal perfumes."

She was unwilling to bid the gentleman rise and go, because this was the Lady Mary's room.

"Where your Grace is, there the spring abideth," Mary said sardonically. "*Ecce miraculum sicut erat, Joshuâ rege.*"

The little Prince came timidly down to beg a flower from the Queen and they all had their backs upon the spy. He ran his hands down his beard and considered the Queen's words. Then swiftly he was on his feet and through the door. He was more ready to brave the Lady Mary's after-wrath than let the Queen see him upon his knees. For actually it was a treason to kneel to the Lady Mary. It had been proclaimed so in the old days when the King's daughter was always subject to new debasements. And who knew whether now the penalty of treason might not still be enacted? It was certain that the Queen had no liking for the Archbishop. Then, what use might she not make of the fact that the Archbishop's man knelt, seeming to curry favour, though in these days all men knelt to her, even when the King was by? He cursed himself as he hastened away.

The Queen looked over her shoulder and caught the glint of his red heel as it went past the doorpost.

"In our north parts," she said, and she was glad that Lascelles had fled, "the seasons come ever tardily."

"Well, your Grace has not delayed to blossom," Mary said.

It was part of her humour when she was in a taunting mood to call the Queen always "your Grace" or "your Majesty" at every turn of the phrase.

Katharine looked at the pink intently. Her face had no expression, she was determined at once to have a cheerful patience and not to show it in her face.

The little Prince stole his hand into hers.

"Wherefore did my father—*rex pater meus*—pummel the man in the long cloak?" he asked.

"You knew it then?" Katharine asked of her stepdaughter.

"I knew it not," the Lady Mary answered.

"I saw it from this window, but my sister would not look," the Prince said.

The Queen was going to shut, with her own hand, the door, the little boy trotting behind her, but, purple-clothed and huge, the King was there.

"Well, I will not be shut out in mine own castle," he said pleasantly.

In those, the quiet days of his realm when most things were going well, his face beneath his beard had taken a rounder and a smoother outline. He moved with motions less hasty than those he had had two years before, and when he had cast a task off it was done with and went out of his mind, so that he appeared a very busy man with, between whiles, the leisure to saunter.

"In a half hour," he said, "I go north to meet the King o' Scots. I would I had not the long journey to make but could stay with ye. It is pleasant here; the air is livening." He caught his little son by the armpits and hoisted him on to his purple shoulders. "Hey, princekin," he said, "what news ha' you o' the day?"

The little Edward pulled his father's bonnet off that he might the better see the huge brows and the little eyes.

"I told my sister that you did pummel a man in a long gown. What is even 'long gown' in the learned tongue?" He played daintily and languidly with the hair of the King's temples, and when the King had said that he might call it "*doctorum toga*," he added, "But my sister would not come to look."

"Well, thy sister is a monstrous learned wench," the King said with a heavy benignity. "She could not leave her book."

The Lady Mary stood rigid, with a mock humility. She had her hands clasped before her, the folds of her black skirt fell stiffly just to the ground. She pursed her lips and strove with herself to speak, for she was minded to exhibit disdain, but her black mood was too strong for her.

"I did not read in my book, because I could not," she said numbly. "Your son disturbed my reading. But I did not come to look, because I would not."

With one arm round the boy's little waist as he sat on high, and one hand on the little feet, the King looked at his daughter in a sudden hot rage; for to speak contemptuously of his son was a thing that filled him with anger and surprise. He opened his mouth to shout. Katharine Howard was gently turning a brass sphere with the constellations upon it that stood upon the table. She moved her fair face round towards the King and set her finger upon her lips. He shrugged his shoulders, prince and all moving up together, and his face took on the expression, half abashed and half resigned, of a man who is reminded by his womankind that he is near to a passionate folly.

Katharine by that time had schooled him how to act when Mary was in that humour, and he let out no word.

"I do not like that this Prince should play in my room," the Lady Mary pursued him relentlessly, and he was so well lessoned that he answered only—

"Ye must fight that cock with Kat. It is Kat that sends him, not I."

Nevertheless he was too masterful a man to keep his silence altogether; he was, besides, so content upon the whole that he was sure he could hold his temper in check, and the better to take breath for a long speech, he took the little boy from his shoulder and planted his feet abroad on the carpet.

"See now, Moll," he said, "make friends!" and he stretched out a large hand. She shrugged her shoulders half invisibly.

"I will kneel down to the King of this country and to the Supreme Head of the Church as it is here set up by law. What more would you have of me?"

"See now, Moll!" he said.

He fingered the medal upon his chest and cast about for words.

"Let us have peace in this realm," he said. "We are very near it."

She raised her eyelids with a tiny contempt.

"It hangs much around you," he went on. "Listen! I will tell ye the whole matter."

Slowly and sagaciously he disentangled all his coil of policies. His letter to the Holy Father was all drafted and ready to be put into fine words. But, before he sent it, he must be sure of peace abroad. It was like this—

"Ye know," he said, "though great wrangles have been in the past betwixt him and thee and mine own self, how my heart has ever been well inclined to my nephew, thy cousin the Emperor. There are in Christendom now only he and France that are anyways strong to stand against me or to invade me. But France I ha' never loved, and him much."

"Ye are grown gentle then," Mary said, "and forgiving in your old age, for ye know I ha' plotted against you with my cousin and my cousin with me."

"It is a very ancient tale," the King said. "Forget it, as do I and he."

"Why, you live in the sun where the dial face moves. I in the shadow where Time stays still. To me it is every day a new tale," the Lady Mary answered.

His face took on an expression of patience and resignation that angered her, for she knew that when her father looked so it was always very difficult to move him.

"Why, all the world forgets," he said.

"Save only I," she answered. "I had only one parent—a mother. She is dead: she was done to death."

"I have pardoned your cousin that he plotted against me," he stuck to his tale, "and he me what I did against your mother."

"Well, he was ever a popinjay," the Lady Mary said.

"Lately," Henry continued, "as ye wiz he had grown very thick with Francis of France. He went across the French country into the Netherlands, so strict was their alliance. It is more than I would do to trust myself to France's word. All Holland marvelled."

"What is this to me?" the Lady Mary said. "Will you send me across France to the Netherlands?"

He left her gibe alone.

"But in these latter months," he said, "Kat and I ha' weakened with true messages and loyal conceits this unholy alliance."

"Why, I ha' heard," Mary said, "ye did send the Duke of Norfolk to tell the King o' France that my cousin had said in private that he was the greater King of the twain. These be princely princes!"

"An unholy alliance it was," Henry went on his way, "for the Emperor is a very good Christian and a loyal son of the Church. But Francis worships the devil—I have heard it said and I believe it—or, at least, he believes not in God and our Saviour; and he pays allegiance to the

Church only when it serves his turn, now holding on, now letting go. I am glad this alliance is dissolving."

"Why, I am glad to hear you speak like this," Mary said bitterly. "You are a goodly son to Mother Church."

The King took her scorn with a shrug of the shoulders.

"I am glad this alliance is dissolved or dissolving," he said, "for when it is fully dissolved I will make my peace with Rome. And I long for that day, for I am weary of errors."

"Well, this is a very goodly tale," Mary said. "I am glad you are minded to escape hell-flame. What is it all to me?"

"The burden of it rests with thee," he answered, "for thou alone canst make thy cousin believe in my true mind."

"God help me," Mary said.

"See you, Moll," the King broke in on her eagerly, "if you will marry the Infant of Spain—"

"God's sakes," she said lightly, "my cousin's son will wed no bastard as I be."

He brushed her jest aside with one hand.

"See you," he said, "now I ride to the north to meet the King o' Scots. That nephew of mine has always been too thick with Francis. But I will be so friendly with him. And see you, with the Scots cut away and the Emperor unloyal, the teeth of Francis are drawn. I might not send my letter to the Pope with all Christendom arrayed together against me. But when they are set by the ears I am strong enow."

"Oh, good!" the Lady Mary said. "Strong enow to be humble!"

Her eyes sparkled so much and her bosom so heaved, that Katharine moved solicitously and swiftly to come between them.

"See you, Moll," the King said, "forgive the ill I wrought thee, and so shall golden days come again. Once more there shall be a deep peace with contented husbandmen and the spreading of the vines abroad upon the stakes. And once more *venite creator spiritus* shall be sung in this land. And once more you shall be much honoured; nay, you shall be as one that saved this realm—"

She screamed out—

"Stay your tongue!" with such a shrill voice that the King's words were drowned. Katharine Howard ran in between them, but she pushed her aside, speaking over her shoulder.

"Before God," she said, "you gar me forget that you are the King that begot me illegally."

Katharine turned upon the King and sought to move him from the room. But he was still of opinion that he could convince his daughter and stood his ground, looking over her shoulder as Mary had done.

"Body of God!" Mary said. "Body of God! That a man could deem me so base!" She looked, convulsed, into Henry's eyes. "Can you bring my mother alive by the truckling and cajoling and setting lying prince against lying prince? You slew my mother by lies, or your man slew her by poison. It is all one. And will you come to me that you have decreed misbegotten, to help you save your soul!"

There was such a violent hatred in her tone that the King could bring no word out, and she swept on—

"Could even a man be such a dull villain? To creep into heaven by bribing his daughter! To creep into heaven by strengthening himself with lies about one prince to another till he be strong enow to be humble! This is a king! This is even a man! I would be ashamed of such manhood!"

She took a deep breath.

"What can you bribe me with? A marriage with my cousin's son? Why, he has deserted my mother's cause. I had rather wed a falconer than that prince. You will have me no longer called bastard? Why, I had rather be called bastard than the acknowledged child of such a royal King. You will cover me with brocades and set me on high? By God, the sun in the heaven has looked upon such basenesses that I seek only a patch of shade. God help me; you will recall the decree that said my mother was not a Queen! God help us! God help us all! You will ennoble my mother's memory. With a decree! Can all the decrees you can make render my mother more sacred? When you decreed her not a Queen, did a soul believe it? If now you decree that a Queen she was, who will believe you? I think I had rather you left it alone, it is such a foul thing to have been thy wife!"

The saying of these things had pleased her so much that she gained control of her tongue.

"You cannot bribe me," she said calmly. "You have naught to give that I have need of."

But the King was so used to his daughter's speeches that, though he had seldom seen her so mutinous, he could still ignore them.

"Well," he said, "I think you are angered with me for having set the Magister in gaol—"

"And in addition," the Lady Mary pursued her own speech, for she deemed that she had thought of a thing to pain both him and the

Queen, "how might I with a good conscience tell my cousin that you have a true inclination to him? I do believe you have; it is this lady that has given it you. But how much longer will this lady sway you? No doubt the King o' Scots hath a new lady for you—and she will be on the French side, for the King o' Scots is the French King's man."

The King opened his mouth convulsively, but Katharine Howard laid her hand right across it.

"You must be riding soon," she said. "I have had a collation set in my chamber." She was so used by now to the violent humours of these Tudors. "You have still to direct me," she added, "what is to be done with these rived cattle."

As they went through the door, the little Prince holding his father's hand and she moving him gently by the shoulder, the child said—

"I thought ye wad ha' little profit speaking to my sister in her then mood."

The King, in the gallery, looked with a gentle apprehension at his wife.

"I trow ye think I ha' done wrong," he said.

She answered—

"Oh nay; she must come to know one day what your Grace had to tell her. Now it is over. But I would not have had you heated. For it is ill to start riding in a sweat. You shall not go for an hour yet."

That pleased him, for it made him think she was unwilling he should go.

In her own room the Lady Mary sat back in her chair and smiled grimly at the ceiling.

"Body of God," she said, "I wish he had married this wench or ever he saw my mother." Nevertheless, upon reflection, she got pleasure from the thought that her mother, with her Aragonia pride, had given the King some ill hours before he had put her away to her death. Katharine of Aragon had been no Katharine Howard to study her lord's ways and twist him about her finger; and Mary took her rosary from a nail beside her and told her beads for a quarter hour to calm herself.

V

There fell upon the castle a deep peace when the King and most of the men were gone. The Queen had the ordering of all things in the castle and of most in the realm. Beneath her she had the Archbishop and some few of the lords of the council who met most days round a long table in the largest hall, and afterwards brought her many papers to sign or to approve. But they were mostly papers of accounts for the castles that were then building, and some few letters from the King's envoys in foreign courts. Upon the whole, there was little stirring, though the Emperor Charles V was then about harrying the Protestant Princes of Almain and Germany. That was good enough news, and though the great castle had well-nigh seven hundred souls, for the most part women, in it, yet it appeared to be empty. High up upon the upper battlements the guards kept a lazy watch. Sometimes the Queen rode a-hawking with her ladies and several lords; when it rained she held readings from the learned writers amongst her ladies, to teach them Latin better. For she had set a fashion of good learning among women that did not for many years die out of the land. In that pursuit she missed the Magister Udal, for the ladies listened to him more willingly than to another. They were reading the *True History of Lucian*, which had been translated into Latin from the Greek about that time.

What occupied her most was the writing of the King's letter to the Pope. Down in their cellar the Archbishop and Lascelles wrought many days at this very long piece of writing. But they made it too humble to suit her, for she would not have her lord to crawl, as if in the dust upon his belly, so she told the Archbishop. Henry was to show contrition and repentance, desire for pardon and the promise of amendment. But he was a very great King and had wrought greatly. And, having got the draft of it in the vulgar tongue, she set about herself to turn it into Latin, for she esteemed herself the best Latinist that they had there.

But in that again she missed the Magister at last, and in the end she sent for him up from his prison to her ante-chamber where it pleased her to sit. It was a tall, narrow room, with much such a chair and dais as were in the room of the Lady Mary. It gave on to her bedchamber that was larger, and it had little, bright, deep windows in the thick walls. From them there could be seen nothing but the blue sky, it was so high up. Here she sat, most often with the Lady Rochford, upon a little stool writing, with the parchments upon her knee or setting a maid to sew. The King had lately made her a gift of twenty-four satin quilts. Most of her maids sat in her painted gallery, carding and spinning wool, but usually she did not sit with them, since she was of opinion that they spoke more freely and took more pleasure when she was not there. She had brought many maids with her into Yorkshire for this spinning, for she believed that this northern wool was the best that could be had. Margot Poins sat always with these maids to keep them to their tasks, and her brother had been advanced to keep the Queen's door when she was in her private rooms, being always without the chamber in which she sat.

When the Magister came to her, she had with her in the little room the Lady Rochford and the Lady Cicely Rochford that had married the old knight when she was Cicely Elliott. Udal had light chains on his wrists and on his ankles, and the Queen sent her guards to await him at her outer door. The Lady Cicely set back her head and laughed at the ceiling.

"Why, here are the bonds of holy matrimony!" she said to his chains. "I ha' never seen them so plain before."

The Magister had straws on his cloak, and he limped a little, being stiff with the damp of his cell.

"*Ave, Regina!*" he said. "*Moriturus te saluto!*" He sought to kneel, but he could not bend his joints; he smiled with a humorous and rueful countenance at his own plight.

The Queen said she had brought him there to read the Latin of her letter. He ducked his brown, lean head.

"*Ha,*" he said, "*sine cane pastor*—without his dog, as Lucretius hath it, the shepherd watches in vain. Wolves—videlicet, errors—shall creep into your marshalled words."

Katharine kept to him a cold face and, a little abashed, he muttered under his breath—

"I ha' played with many maids, but this is the worst pickle that ever I was in."

He took her parchment and read, but, because she was the Queen, he would not say aloud that he found solecisms in her words.

"Give me," he said, "your best pen, and let me sit upon a stool!"

He sat down upon the stool, set the writing on his knee, and groaned with his stiffness. He took up his task, but when those ladies began to talk—the Lady Cicely principally about a hawk that her old knight had training for the Queen, a white sea hawk from Norway—he winced and hissed a little because they disturbed him.

"Misery!" he said; "I remember the days when no mouse dared creak if I sat to my task in the learned tongues."

The Queen then remembered very well how she had been a little girl with the Magister for tutor in her father's great and bare house. It was after Udal had been turned out of his mastership at Eton. He had been in vile humour in most of those days, and had beaten her very often and fiercely with his bundle of twigs. It was only afterwards that he had called her his best pupil.

Remembering these things, she dropped her voice and sat still, thinking. Cicely Elliott, who could not keep still, blew a feather into the air and caught it again and again. The old Lady Rochford, her joints swollen with rheumatism, played with her beads in her lap. From time to time she sighed heavily and, whilst the Magister wrote, he sighed after her. Katharine would not send her ladies away, because she would not be alone with him to have him plague her with entreaties. She would not go herself, because it would have been to show him too much honour then, though a few days before she would have gone willingly because his vocation and his knowledge of the learned tongues made him a man that it was right to respect.

But when she read what he had written for her, his lean, brown face turning eagerly and with a ferreting motion from place to place on the parchment, she was filled with pity and with admiration for the man's talent. It was as if Seneca were writing to his master, or Pliny to the Emperor Trajan. And, being a very tender woman at bottom—

"Magister," she said, "though you have wrought me the greatest grief I think ye could, by so injuring one I like well, yet this is to me so great a service that I will entreat the King to remit some of your pains."

He stumbled up from his stool and this time managed to kneel.

"Oh, Queen," he said, "*Doctissima fuisti*; you were the best pupil that ever I had—" She tried to silence him with a motion of her hand. But he twined his lean hands together with the little chains hanging from them. "I call this to your pitiful mind," he brought out, "not because I would have you grateful, but to make you mindful of what I suffer—*non quia grata sed ut clemens sis*. For, for advancement I have no stomach, since by advancing me you will advance my wife from Paris, and for liberty I have no use since you may never make me free of her. Leave me to rot in my cell, but, if it be but the tractate of Diodorus Siculus, a very dull piece, let me be given some book in a learned tongue. I faint, I starve, I die for lack of good letters. I that no day in my life have passed—*nulla die sine*—no day without reading five hours in goodly books since I was six and breeched. Bethink you, you that love learning—"

"Now tell me," Cicely Elliott cried out, "which would you rather in your cell—the Letters of Cicero or a kitchen wench?"

The Queen bade her hold her peace, and to the Magister she uttered—

"Books I will have sent you, for I think it well that you should be so well employed. And, for your future, I will have you set down in a monastery where there shall be for you much learning and none of my sex. You have done harm enow! Now, get you gone!"

He sighed that she had grown so stern, and she was glad to be rid of him. But he had not been gone a minute into the other room when there arose such a clamour of harsh voices and shrieks and laughter that she threw her door open, coming to it herself before the other ladies could close their mouths, which had opened in amazement.

The young Poins was beating the Magister, so that the fur gown made a greyish whirl about his scarlet suit in the midst of a tangle of spun wool; spinning wheels were overset, Margot Poins crashed around upon them, wailing; the girls with their distaffs were crouching against the window-places and in corners, crying out each one of them.

The Queen had a single little gesture of the hand with which she dismissed all her waiting-women. She stood alone in the inner doorway with the Lady Cicely and the Lady Rochford behind her. The Lady Rochford wrung her gouty hands; the Lady Cicely set back her head and laughed.

The Queen spoke no word, but in the new silence it was as if the Magister fell out of the boy's hands. He staggered amidst the trails of wool, nearly fell, and then made stiff zigzags towards the open outer door, where his prison guards awaited him, since they had no warrant to enter the antechamber. He dragged after him a little trail of fragments of spinning wheels and spindles.

"Well, there's a fine roister-doister!" the Lady Cicely laughed behind the Queen's back. The Queen stood very still and frowned. To her the disturbance was monstrous and distasteful, for she was minded to have things very orderly and quiet. The boy, in his scarlet, pulled off his bonnet and panted, but he was not still more than a second, and suddenly he called out to the Queen—

"Make that pynot to marry my sister!"

Margot Poins hung round him and cried out—

"Oh no! Oh no!"

He shook her roughly loose.

"An' you do not wed with him how shall I get advancement?" he said. "'A promised me that when 'a should come to be Chancellor 'a would advance me."

He pushed her from him again with his elbow when she came near.

"Y've grown over familiar," the Queen said, "with being too much near me. Y'are grown over familiar. For seven days you shall no longer keep my door."

Margot Poins raised her arms over her head, then she leant against a window-pane and sobbed into the crook of her elbow. The boy's slender face was convulsed with rage; his blue eyes started from his head; his callow hair was crushed up.

"Shall a man—" he began to protest.

"I say nothing against that you did beat this Magister," the Queen said. "Such passions cannot be controlled, and I pass it by."

"But will ye not make this man to wed with my sister?" the boy said harshly.

"I cannot. He hath a wedded wife!"

He dropped his hands to his side.

"Alack; then my father's house is down," he cried out.

"Gentleman Guard," Katharine said, "get you for seven days away from my door. I will have another sentry whilst you bethink you of a worthier way to advancement."

He gazed at her stupidly.

"You will not make this wedding?" he asked.

"Gentleman Guard," Katharine said, "you have your answer. Get you gone."

A sudden rage came into his eyes; he swallowed in his throat and made a gesture of despair with his hand. The Queen turned back into her room and busied herself with her task, which was the writing into a little vellum book of seven prayers to the Virgin that the Lady Elizabeth, Queen Anne Boleyn's daughter, a child then in London, was to turn each one into seven languages, written fair in the volume as a gift, against Christmas, for the King.

"I would not have that boy to guard my door," the Lady Cicely said to the Queen.

"Why, 'tis a good boy," Katharine answered; "and his sister loves me very well."

"Get your Highness another," the Lady Cicely persisted. "I do not like his looks."

The Queen gazed up from her writing to where the dark girl, her figure raked very much back in her stiff bodice, played daintily with the tassels of the curtain next the window.

"My Lady," Katharine said, "my Highness must get me a new maid in place of Margot Poins, that shall away into a nunnery. Is not that grief enough for poor Margot? Shall she think in truth that she has undone her father's house?"

"Then advance the springald to some post away from you," the Lady Cicely said.

"Nay," the Queen answered; "he hath done nothing to merit advancement."

She continued, with her head bent down over the writing on her knee, her lips moving a little as, sedulously, she drew large and plain letters with her pen.

"By Heaven," the Lady Cicely said, "you have too tickle a conscience to be a Queen of this world and day. In the time of Cæsar you might have lived more easily."

The Queen looked up at her from her writing; her clear eyes were untroubled.

"Aye," she said. "*Lucio Domitio, Appio Claudio consulibus—*"

Cicely Rochford set back her head and laughed at the ceiling.

"Aye, your Highness is a Roman," she tittered like a magpie.

"In the day of Cæsar it was simple to do well," the Queen said.

"Why, I do not believe it," Cicely answered her.

"Cousin! Cousin!" The old Lady Rochford warned her that this was the Queen, not her old playmate.

"But now," the Queen said, "with such a coming together and a concourse of peoples about us; with such holes and corners in a great Court—" She paused and sighed.

"Well, if I may not speak my mind," Cicely Rochford said to the old lady, "what good am I?"

"I did even what I might to keep this lamb Margot from the teeth of that wolf Magister," the Queen said. "I take shame to myself that I did no more. I will do a penance for it. But still I think that these be degenerate days."

"Oh, Queen of dreams and fancies," Cicely Rochford said. "I am very certain that in the days of your noble Romans it was as it is now. Tell me, if you can, that in all your readings of hic and hoc you lit not upon such basenesses? You will not lay your hand upon your heart and say that never a man of Rome bartered his sister for the hope of advancement, or that never a learned doctor was a corrupter of youth? I have seen the like in the plays of Plautus that here have been played at Court."

"Why," the Queen said, "the days of Plautus were days degenerated and fallen already from the ancient nobleness."

"You should have Queened it before Goodman Adam fell," Cicely Rochford mocked her. "If you go back before Plautus, go back all the way."

She shrugged her shoulders up to her ears and uttered a little sound like "*Pfui!*" Then she said quickly—

"Give me leave to be gone, your Highness, that I may not grow over familiar like the boy with the pikestaff, for if it do not gall you it shall wring the withers of this my old husband's cousin!"

The old Lady Rochford, who was always thinking of what had been said two speeches ago, because she was so slow-witted, raised her gouty hands in the air and opened her mouth. But the Queen smiled faintly at Cicely.

"When I ask you to mince matters in my little room you shall do it. It was Lucius the Praetor that went always accompanied by a carping Stoic to keep him from being puffed up, and it was a good custom."

"Before Heaven," Cicely Rochford said in the midst of her curtsey at the door, "shall I have the office of such a one as Diogenes who derided Alexander the Emperor? Then must my old husband live with me in a tub!"

"Pray you," the Queen said after her through the door, "look you around and spy me out a maid to be my tiring-woman and ward my spinsters. For nowadays I see few maids to choose from."

When she was gone the old Lady Rochford timorously berated the Queen. She would have her be more distant with knights' wives and the like. For it was fitting for a Queen to be feared and deemed awful.

"I had rather be loved and deemed pitiful," Katharine answered. "For I was once such a one—no more—than she or thou, or very little more. Before the people I bear myself proudly for my lord his high honour.

But I do lead a very cloistered life, and have leisure to reflect upon for what a little space authority endureth, and how that friendship and true love between friends are things that bear the weather better." She did not say her Latin text, for the old lady had no Latin.

VI

In the underground cell, above the red and gold table that afternoon, Lascelles wrought at a fair copy of the King's letter to the Pope, amended as it had been by Udal's hand. The Archbishop had come into the room reading a book as he came from his prayers, and sate him down in his chair at the tablehead without glancing at his gentleman.

"Prithee, your Grace," Lascelles said, "suffer me to carry this letter mine own self to the Queen."

The Archbishop looked up at him; his mournful eyes started wide; he leaned forward.

"Art thou Lascelles?" he asked.

"Aye, Lascelles I am," the gentleman answered; "but I have cut off my beard."

The Archbishop was very weak and startled; he fell into an anger.

"Is this a time for vanities?" he said. "Will you be after the wenches? You look a foolish boy! I do not like this prank."

Lascelles put up his hand to stroke his vanished beard. His risible lips writhed in a foxy smile; his chin was fuller than you would have expected, round and sensuous with a dimple in the peak of it.

"Please it, your Grace," he said, "this is no vanity, but a scheme that I will try."

"What scheme? What scheme?" the Archbishop said. "Here have been too many schemes." He was very shaken and afraid, because this world was beyond his control.

"Please it, your Grace," Lascelles answered, "ask me not what this scheme is."

The Archbishop shook his head and pursed his lips feebly.

"Please it, your Grace," Lascelles urged, "if this scheme miscarry, your Grace shall hear no more of it. If this scheme succeed I trow it shall help some things forward that your Grace would much have forwarded. Please it, your Grace, to ask me no more, and to send me with this letter to the Queen's Highness."

The Archbishop opened his nerveless hands before him; they were pale and wrinkled as if they had been much soddened in water. Since the King had bidden him compose that letter to the Pope of Rome, his hands had grown so. Lascelles wrote on at the new draft of the letter, his lips following the motions of his pen. Still writing, and with his eyes down, he said—

"The Queen's Highness will put from her her tirewoman in a week from now."

The Archbishop moved his fingers as who should say—

"What is that to me!" His eyes gazed into the space above his book that lay before him on the table.

"This Margot Poins is a niece of the master-printer Badge, a Lutheran, of the Austin Friars." Lascelles pursued his writing for a line further. Then he added—

"This putting away and the occasion of it shall make a great noise in the town of London. It will be said amongst the Lutherans that the Queen is answerable therefor. It will be said that the Queen hath a very lewd Court and companionship."

The Archbishop muttered wearily—

"It hath been said already."

"But not," Lascelles said, "since she came to be Queen."

The Archbishop directed upon him his hang-dog eyes, and his voice was the voice of a man that would not be disturbed from woeful musings.

"What use?" he said bitterly; and then again, "What use?"

Lascelles wrote on sedulously. He used his sandarach to the end of the page, blew off the sand, eyed the sheet sideways, laid it down, and set another on his writing-board.

"Why," he brought out quietly, "it may be brought to the King's Highness' ears."

"What way?" the Archbishop said heavily, as if the thing were impossible. His gentleman answered—

"This way and that!" The King's Highness had a trick of wandering about among his faithful lieges unbeknown; foreign ambassadors wrote abroad such rumours which might be re-reported from the foreign by the King's servants.

"Such a report," Lascelles said, "hath gone up already to London town by a swift carrier."

The Archbishop brought out wearily and distastefully—

"How know you? Was it you that wrote it?"

"Please it, your Grace," his gentleman answered him, "it was in this wise. As I was passing by the Queen's chamber wall I heard a great outcry—"

He laid down his pen beside his writing-board the more leisurely to speak.

He had seen Udal, beaten and shaking, stagger out from the Queen's door to where his guards waited to set him back in prison. From Udal he had learned of this new draft of the letter; of Udal's trouble he knew before. Udal gone, he had waited a little, hearing the Queen's voice and what she said very plainly, for the castle was very great and quiet. Then out had come the young Poins, breathing like a volcano through his nostrils, and like to be stricken with palsy, boy though he was. Him Lascelles had followed at a convenient distance, where he staggered and snorted. And, coming upon the boy in an empty guard-room near the great gate, he had found him aflame with passion against the Queen's Highness.

"I," the boy had cried out, "I that by my carrying of letters set this Howard where she sits! I!—and this is my advancement. My sister cast down, and I cast out, and another maid to take my sister's place."

And Lascelles, in the guard-chamber, had shown him sympathy and reminded him that there was gospel for saying that princes had short memories.

"But I did not calm him!" Lascelles said.

On the contrary, upon Lascelles' suggestion that the boy had but to hold his tongue and pocket his wrongs, the young Poins had burst out that he would shout it all abroad at every street corner. And suddenly it had come into his head to write such a letter to his Uncle Badge the printer as, printed in a broadside, would make the Queen's name to stink, until the last generation was of men, in men's nostrils.

Lascelles rubbed his hands gently and sinuously together. He cast one sly glance at the Archbishop.

"Well, the letter was written," he said. "Be sure the broadside shall be printed."

Cranmer's head was sunk over his book.

"This lad," Lascelles said softly, "who in seven days' time again shall keep the Queen's door (for it is not true that the Queen's Highness is an ingrate, well sure am I), this lad shall be a very useful confidant; a very serviceable guide to help us to a knowledge of who goes in to the Queen and who cometh out."

The Archbishop did not appear to be listening to his gentleman's soft voice and, resuming his pen, Lascelles finished his tale with—

"For I have made this lad my friend. It shall cost me some money, but I do not doubt that your Grace shall repay."

The Archbishop raised his head.

"No, before God in heaven on His throne!" he said. His voice was shrill and high; he agitated his hands in their fine, tied sleeves. "I will have no part in these Cromwell tricks. All is lost; let it be lost. I must say my prayers."

"Has it been by saying of your Grace's prayers that your Grace has lived through these months?" Lascelles asked softly.

"Aye," the Archbishop wrung his hands; "you girded me and moved me when Cromwell lay at death, to write a letter to the King's Highness. To write such a letter as should appear brave and faithful and true to Privy Seal's cause."

"Such a letter your Grace wrote," Lascelles said; "and it was the best writing that ever your Grace made."

The Archbishop gazed at the table.

"How do I know that?" he said in a whisper. "You say so, who bade me write it."

"For that your Grace lives yet," Lascelles said softly; "though in those days a warrant was written for your capture. For, sure it is, and your Grace has heard it from the King's lips, that your letter sounded so faithful and piteous and true to him your late leader, that the King could not but believe that you, so loyal in such a time to a man disgraced and cast down beyond hope, could not but be faithful and loyal in the future to him, the King, with so many bounties to bestow."

"Aye," the Archbishop said, "but how do I know what of a truth was in the King's mind who casteth down today one, tomorrow another, till none are left?"

And again Cranmer dropped his anguished eyes to the table.

IN THOSE DAYS STILL—AND he slept still worse since the King had bidden him write this letter to Rome—the Archbishop could not sleep on any night without startings and sweats and cryings out in his sleep. And he gave orders that, when he so cried out, the page at his bedside should wake him.

For then he was seeing the dreadful face of his great master, Privy Seal, when the day of his ruin had come. Cromwell had been standing in a window of the council chamber at Westminster looking out upon a courtyard. In behind him had come the other lords of the council, Norfolk with his yellow face, the High Admiral, and many others; and each, seating himself at the table, had kept his bonnet on his head.

So Cromwell, turning, had seen them and had asked with his hard insolence and embittered eyes of hatred, how they dared be covered before he who was their president sat down. Then, up against him in the window-place there had sprung Norfolk at the chain of the George round his neck, and Suffolk at the Garter on his knee; and Norfolk had cried out that Thomas Cromwell was no longer Privy Seal of that kingdom, nor president of that council, but a traitor that must die. Then such rage and despair had come into Thomas Cromwell's terrible face that Cranmer's senses had reeled. He had seen Norfolk and the Admiral fall back before this passion; he had seen Thomas Cromwell tear off his cap and cast it on the floor; he had heard him bark and snarl out certain words into the face of the yellow dog of Norfolk.

"*Upon your life you dare not call me traitor!*" and Norfolk had fallen back abashed.

Then the chamber had seemed to fill with an awful gloom and darkness; men showed only like shadows against the window lights; the constable of the Tower had come in with the warrants, and in that gloom the earth had appeared to tremble and quake beneath the Archbishop's feet.

HE CROSSED HIMSELF AT THE recollection, and, coming out of his stupor, saw that Lascelles was finishing his writings. And he was glad that he was here now and not there then.

"Prithee, your Grace," the gentleman's soft voice said, "let me bear, myself, this letter to the Queen."

The Archbishop shivered frostily in his robes.

"I will have no more Cromwell tricks," he said. "I have said it"; and he affected an obdurate tone.

"Then, indeed, all is lost," Lascelles answered; "for this Queen is very resolved."

The Archbishop cast his eyes up to the cold stone ceiling above him. He crossed himself.

"You are a very devil," he said, and panic came into his eyes, so that he turned them all round him as if he sought an issue at which to run out.

"The Papist lords in this castle met on Saturday night," Lascelles said; "their meeting was very secret, and Norfolk was their head. But I have heard it said that not one of them was for the Queen."

The Archbishop shrank within himself.

"I am not minded to hear this," he said.

"Not one of them was for the Queen altogether; for she will render all lands and goods back to the Church, and there is no one of them but is rich with the lands and goods of the Church. That they that followed Cromwell are not for the Queen well your Grace knoweth," his gentleman continued.

"I will not hear this; this is treason," the Archbishop muttered.

"So that who standeth for the Queen?" Lascelles whispered. "Only a few of the baser sort that have no lands to lose."

"The King," the Archbishop cried out in a terrible voice; "the King standeth for her!"

He sprang up in his chair and then sank down again, covering his mouth with his hands, as if he would have intercepted the uttered words. For who knew who listened at what doors in these days. He whispered horribly—

"What a folly is this. Who shall move the King? Will reports of his ambassadors that Cleves, or Charles, or Francis miscall the Queen? You know they will not, for the King is aware of how these princes batten on carrion. Will broad sheets of the Lutheran? You know they will not, for the King is aware of how those coggers come by their tales. Will the King go abroad among the people any more to hear what they say? You know he will not. For he is grown too old, and his fireside is made too sweet—"

He wavered, and he could not work himself up with a longer show of anger.

"Prithee," Lascelles said, "let me bear this letter myself to the Queen." His voice was patient and calm.

The Archbishop lay back, impotent, in his chair. His arms were along the arms of it: he had dropped his book upon the table. His long gown was draped all over him down to his feet; his head remained motionless; his eyes did not wink, and gazed at despair; his hands drooped, open and impotent.

Suddenly he moved one of them a very little.

VII

It was the Queen's habit to go every night, when the business of the day was done, to pray, along with the Lady Mary, in the small chapel that was in the roof of the castle. To vespers she went with all the Court to the big chapel in the courtyard that the King had builded especially for her. But to this little chapel, that was of Edward IV's time, small and round-arched, all stone and dark and bare, she went with the Lady Mary alone. Her ladies and her doorguards they left at the stair foot, on a level with the sleeping rooms of the poorer sort, but up the little stairway they climbed by themselves, in darkness, to pray privately for the conversion of England. For this little place was so small and so forgotten that it had never been desecrated by Privy Seal's men. It had had no vessels worth the taking, and only very old vestments and a few ill-painted pictures on the stone walls that were half hidden in the dust.

Katharine had found this little place when, on her first day at Pontefract, she had gone a-wandering over the castle with the King. For she was curious to know how men had lived in the old times; to see their rooms and to mark what old things were there still in use. And she had climbed thus high because she was minded to gaze upon the huge expanse of country and of moors that from the upper leads of the castle was to be seen. But this little chapel had seemed to her to be all the more sacred because it had been undesecrated and forgotten. She thought that you could not find such another in the King's realm at that time; she was very assured that not one was to be found in any house of the King's and hers.

And, making inquiries, she had found that there was also an old priest there served the chapel, doing it rather secretly for the well-disposed of the castle's own guards. This old man had fled, at the approach of the King's many, into the hidden valleys of that countryside, where still the faith lingered and lingers now. For, so barbarous and remote those north parts were, that a great many people had never heard that the King was married again, and fewer still, or none, knew that he and his wife were well inclined again towards Rome.

This old priest she had had brought to her. And he was so well loved that along with him came a cluster of weather-battered moorsmen, right with him into her presence. They kneeled down, being clothed with skins, and several of them having bows of a great size, to beg her not to harm this old man, for he was reputed a saint. The Queen could not understand their jargon but, when their suit was interpreted to her by the Lord Dacre of the North, and when she had had a little converse with the old priest, she answered that, so touched was her heart by his simplicity and gentleness, that she would pray the good King, her lord and master, to let this priest be made her confessor whilst there they stayed. And afterwards, if it were convenient, in reward for his faithfulness, he should be made a prior or a bishop in those parts. So the moorsmen, blessing her uncouthly for her fairness and kind words, went back with their furs and bows into their fastnesses. One of them was a great lord of that countryside, and each day he sent into the castle bucks and moor fowl, and once or twice a wolf. His name was Sir John Peel, and Sir John Peel, too, the priest was called.

So the priest served that little altar, and of a night, when the Queen was minded next day to partake of the host, he heard her confession. On other nights he left them there alone to say their prayers. It was always very dark with the little red light burning before the altar and two tapers that they lit beneath a statue of the Virgin, old and black and ill-carved by antique hands centuries before. And, in that blackness, they knelt, invisible almost, and still in the black gowns that they put on for prayers, beside a low pillar that gloomed out at their sides and vanished up into the darkness of the roof.

Having done their prayers, sometimes they stayed to converse and to meditate, for there they could be very private. On the night when the letter to Rome was redrafted, the Queen prayed much longer than the Lady Mary, who sat back upon a stool, silently, to await her finishing— for it seemed that the Queen was more zealous for the converting of those realms again to the old faith than was ever the Lady Mary. The tapers burned with a steady, invisible glow in the little side chapel behind the pillar; the altar gleamed duskily before them, and it was so still that through the unglassed windows they could hear, from far below in the black countryside, a tenuous bleating of late-dropped lambs. Katharine Howard's beads clicked and her dress rustled as she came up from her knees.

"It rests more with thee than with any other in this land," her voice reverberated amongst the distant shadows. A bat that had been drawn in by the light flittered invisibly near them.

"Even what?" the Lady Mary asked.

"Well you know," the Queen answered; "and may the God to whom you have prayed, that softened the heart of Paul, soften thine in this hour!"

The Lady Mary maintained a long silence. The bat flittered, with a leathern rustle, invisible, between their very faces. At last Mary uttered, and her voice was taunting and malicious—

"If you will soften my heart much you must beseech me."

"Why, I will kneel to you," the Queen said.

"Aye, you shall," Mary answered. "Tell me what you would have of me."

"Well you know!" Katharine said again.

In the darkness the lady's voice maintained its bitter mirth, as it were the broken laughter of a soul in anguish.

"I will have you tell me, for it is a shameful tale that will shame you in the telling."

The Queen paused to consider of her words.

"First, you shall be reconciled with, and speak pleasantly with, the King your father and my lord."

"And is it not a shameful thing you bid me do, to bid me speak pleasant words to him that slew my mother and called me bastard?"

The Queen answered that she asked it in the name of Christ, His pitiful sake, and for the good of this suffering land.

"None the less, Queen, thou askest it in the darkness that thy face may not be seen. And what more askest thou?"

"That when the Duke of Orleans his ambassadors come asking your hand in marriage, you do show them a pleasant and acquiescent countenance."

The sacredness of that dark place kept Mary from laughing aloud.

"That, too, you dare not ask in the light of day, Queen," she said. "Ask on!"

"That when the Emperor's ambassadors shall ask for your hand you shall profess yourself glad indeed."

"Well, here is more shame, that I should be prayed to feign this gladness. I think the angels do laugh that hear you. Ask even more."

Katharine said patiently—

"That, having in reward of these favours, been set again on high, having honours shown you and a Court appointed round you, you shall gladly play the part of a princess royal to these realms, never gibing, nor sneering upon this King your father, nor calling upon the memory of the wronged Queen your mother."

"Queen," the Lady Mary said, "I had thought that even in the darkness you had not dared to ask me this."

"I will ask it you again," the Queen said, "in your room where the light of the candles shines upon my face."

"Why, you shall," the Lady Mary said. "Let us presently go there."

THEY WENT DOWN THE DARK and winding stair. At the foot the procession of the *coucher de la royne* awaited them, first being two trumpeters in black and gold, then four pikemen with lanthorns, then the marshal of the Queen's household and five or seven lords, then the Queen's ladies, the Lady Rochford that slept with her, the Lady Cicely Rochford; the Queen's tiring-women, leaving a space between them for the Queen and the Lady Mary to walk in, then four young pages in scarlet and with the Queen's favours in their caps, and then the guard of the Queen's door, and four pikemen with torches whose light, falling from behind, illumined the path for the Queen's steps. The trumpeters blew four shrill blasts and then four with their fists in the trumpet mouths to muffle them. The brazen cries wound down the dark corridors, fathoms and fathoms down, to let men know that the Queen had done her prayers and was going to her bed. This great state was especially devised by the King to do honour to the new Queen that he loved better than any he had had. The purpose of it was to let all men know what she did that she might be the more imitated.

But the Queen bade them guide her to the Lady Mary's door, and in the doorway she dismissed them all, save only her women and her door guard and pikemen who awaited her without, some on stools and some against the wall, ladies and men alike.

The Lady Mary looked into the Queen's face very close and laughed at her when they were in the fair room and the light of the candles.

"Now you shall say your litany over again," she sneered; "I will sit me down and listen." And in her chair at the table, with her face averted, she dug with little stabs into the covering rug the stiletto with which she was wont to mend her pens.

Standing by her, her face fully lit by the many candles that were upon the mantel, the Queen, dressed all in black and with the tail of her hood falling down behind to her feet, went patiently through the list of her prayers—that the Lady Mary should be reconciled with her father, that she should show at first favour to the ambassadors that sued for her hand for the Duke of Orleans, and afterwards give a glad consent to her marriage with the Prince Philip, the Emperor's son; and then, having been reinstated as a princess of the royal house of England, she should bear herself as such, and no more cry out upon the memory of Katharine of Aragon that had been put away from the King's side.

The Queen spoke these words with a serious patience and a level voice; but when she came to the end of them she stretched out her hand and her voice grew full.

"And oh," she said, her face being set and earnest in entreaty towards the girl's back, "if you have any love for the green and fertile land that gave birth both to you and to me—"

"But to me a bastard," the Lady Mary said.

"If you would have the dishoused saints to return home to their loved pastures; if you would have the Mother of God and of us all to rejoice again in her dowry; if you would see a great multitude of souls, gentle and simple reconducted again towards Heaven—"

"Well, well!" the Lady Mary said; "grovel! grovel! I had thought you would have been shamed thus to crawl upon your belly before me."

"I would crawl in the dust," Katharine said. "I would kiss the mire from the shoon of the vilest man there is if in that way I might win for the Church of God—"

"Well, well!" the Lady Mary said.

"You will not let me finish my speech about our Saviour and His mother," the Queen said. "You are afraid I should move you."

The Lady Mary turned suddenly round upon her in her chair. Her face was pallid, the skin upon her hollowed temples trembled—

"Queen," she called out, "ye blaspheme when ye say that a few paltry speeches of yours about God and souls will make me fail my mother's memory and the remembrances of the shames I have had."

She closed her eyes; she swallowed in her throat and then, starting up, she overset her chair.

"To save souls!" she said. "To save a few craven English souls! What are they to me? Let them burn in the eternal fires! Who among them raised a hand or struck a blow for my mother or me? Let them go shivering to hell."

"Lady," the Queen said, "ye know well how many have gone to the stake over conspiracies for you in this realm."

"Then they are dead and wear the martyr's crown," the Lady Mary said. "Let the rest that never aided me, nor struck blow for my mother, go rot in their heresies."

"But the Church of God!" the Queen said. "The King's Highness has promised me that upon the hour when you shall swear to do these things he will send the letter that ye wot of to our Father in Rome."

The Lady Mary laughed aloud—

"Here is a fine woman," she said. "This is ever the woman's part to gloss over crimes of their men folk. What say you to the death of Lady Salisbury that died by the block a little since?"

She bent her body and poked her head forward into the Queen's very face. Katharine stood still before her.

"God knows," she said. "I might not stay it. There was much false witness—or some of it true—against her. I pray that the King my Lord may atone for it in the peace that shall come."

"The peace that shall come!" the Lady Mary laughed. "Oh, God, what things we women are when a man rules us. The peace that shall come? By what means shall it have been brought on?"

"I will tell you," she pursued after a moment. "All this is cogging and lying and feigning and chicaning. And you who are so upright will crawl before me to bring it about. Listen!"

And she closed her eyes the better to calm herself and to collect her thoughts, for she hated to appear moved.

"I am to feign a friendship to my father. That is a lie that you ask me to do, for I hate him as he were the devil. And why must I do this? To feign a smooth face to the world that his pride may not be humbled. I am to feign to receive the ambassadors of the Duke of Orleans. That is cogging that you ask of me. For it is not intended that ever I shall wed with a prince of the French house. But I must lead them on and on till the Emperor be affrighted lest your King make alliance with the French. What a foul tale! And you lend it your countenance!"

"I would well—" Katharine began.

"Oh, I know, I know," Mary snickered. "Ye would well be chaste but that it must needs be other with you. It was the thief's wife said that.

"Listen again," she pursued, "anon there shall come the Emperor's men, and there shall be more cogging and chicaning, and honours shall be given me that I may be bought dear, and petitioning that I should be set in the succession to make them eager. And then, perhaps, it shall all be cried off and a Schmalkaldner prince shall send ambassadors—"

"No, before God," Katharine said.

"Oh, I know my father," Mary laughed at her. "You will keep him tied to Rome if you can. But you could not save the venerable Lady of Salisbury, nor you shall not save him from trafficking with Schmalkaldners and Lutherans if it shall serve his monstrous passions and his vanities. And if he do not this yet he will do other villainies. And you will cosset him in them—to save his hoggish dignity and buttress up his heavy pride. All this you stand there and ask."

"In the name of God I ask it," Katharine said. "There is no other way."

"Well then," the Lady Mary said, "you shall ask it many times. I will have you shamed."

"Day and night I will ask it," Katharine said.

The Lady Mary sniffed.

"It is very well," she said. "You are a proud and virtuous piece. I will humble you. It were nothing to my father to crawl on his belly and humble himself and slaver. He would do it with joy, weeping with a feigned penitence, making huge promises, foaming at the mouth with oaths that he repented, calling me his ever loved child—"

She stayed and then added—

"That would cost him nothing. But that you that are his pride, that you should do it who are in yourself proud—that is somewhat to pay oneself with for shamed nights and days despised. If you will have this thing you shall do some praying for it."

"Even as Jacob served so will I," Katharine said.

"Seven years!" the Lady Mary mocked at her. "God forbid that I should suffer you for so long. I will get me gone with an Orleans, a Kaiserlik, or a Schmalkaldner leaguer before that. So much comfort I will give you." She stopped, lifted her head and said, "One knocks!"

They said from the door that a gentleman was come from the Archbishop with a letter to the Queen's Grace.

VIII

There came in the shaven Lascelles and fell upon his knees, holding up the sheets of the letter he had copied.

The Queen took them from him and laid them upon the great table, being minded later to read them to the Lady Mary, in proof that the King very truly would make his submission to Rome, supposing only that his daughter would make submission to her.

When she turned, Lascelles was still kneeling before the doorway, his eyes upon the ground.

"Why, I thank you," she said. "Gentleman, you may get you gone back to the Archbishop."

She was thinking of returning to her duel of patience with the Lady Mary. But looking upon his blond and agreeable features she stayed for a minute.

"I know your face," she said. "Where have I seen you?"

He looked up at her; his eyes were blue and noticeable, because at times of emotion he was so wide-lidded that the whites showed round the pupils of them.

"Certainly I have seen you," the Queen said.

"It is a royal gift," he said, "the memory of faces. I am the Archbishop's poor gentleman, Lascelles."

The Queen said—

"Lascelles? Lascelles?" and searched her memory.

"I have a sister, the spit and twin of me," he answered; "and her name is Mary."

The Queen said—

"Ah! ah!" and then, "Your sister was my bed-fellow in the maid's room at my grandmother's."

He answered gravely—

"Even so!"

And she—

"Stand up and tell me how your sister fares. I had some kindnesses of her when I was a child. I remember when I had cold feet she would heat a brick in the fire to lay to them, and such tricks. How fares she? Will you not stand up?"

"Because she fares very ill I will not stand upon my feet," he answered.

"Well, you will beg a boon of me," she said. "If it is for your sister I will do what I may with a good conscience."

He answered, remaining kneeling, that he would fain see his sister. But she was very poor, having married an esquire called Hall of these parts, and he was dead, leaving her but one little farm where, too, his old father and mother dwelt.

"I will pay for her visit here," she said; "and she shall have lodging."

"Safe-conduct she must have too," he answered; "for none cometh within seven miles of this court without your permit and approval."

"Well, I will send horses of my own, and men to safeguard her," the Queen said. "For, sure, I am beholden to her in many little things. I think she sewed the first round gown that ever I had."

He remained kneeling, his eyes still upon the floor.

"We are your very good servants, my sister and I," he said. "For she did marry one—that Esquire Hall—that was done to death upon the gallows for the old faith's sake. And it was I that wrote the English of most of this letter to his Holiness, the Archbishop being ill and keeping his bed."

"Well, you have served me very well, it is true," the Queen answered. "What would you have of me?"

"Your Highness," he answered, "I do well love my sister and she me. I would have her given a place here at the Court. I do not ask a great one; not one so high as about your person. For I am sure that you are well attended, and places few there are to spare about you."

And then, even as he willed it, she bethought her that Margot Poins was to go to a nunnery. That afternoon she had decided that Mary Trelyon, who was her second maid, should become her first, and others be moved up in a rote.

"Why," she said, "it may be that I shall find her an occupation. I will not have it said—nor yet do it—that I have ever recompensed them that did me favours in the old times, for there are a many that have served well in the Court that then I was outside of, and those it is fitting first to reward. Yet, since, as you say you have writ the English of this letter, that is a very great service to the Republic, and if by rewarding her I may recompense thee, I will think how I may come to do it."

He stood up upon his feet.

"It may be," he said, "that my sister is rustic and unsuited. I have not seen her in many years. Therefore, I will not pray too high a place for her, but only that she and I may be near, the one to the other, upon occasions, and that she be housed and fed and clothed."

"Why, that is very well said," the Queen answered him. "I will bid my men to make inquiries into her demeanour and behaviour in the place where she bides, and if she is well fitted and modest, she shall have a place about me. If she be too rustic she shall have another place. Get you gone, gentleman, and a good-night to ye."

He bent himself half double, in the then newest courtly way, and still bent, pivoted through the door. The Queen stayed a little while musing.

"Why," she said, "when I was a little child I fared very ill, if now I think of it; but then it seemed a little thing."

"Y'had best forget it," the Lady Mary answered.

"Nay," the Queen said. "I have known too well what it was to go supperless to my bed to forget it. A great shadowy place—all shadows, where the night airs crept in under the rafters."

She was thinking of the maids' dormitory at her grandmother's, the old Duchess.

"I am climbed very high," she said; "but to think—"

She was such a poor man's child and held of only the littlest account, herding with the maids and the servingmen's children. At eight by the clock her grandmother locked her and all the maids—at times there were but ten, at times as many as a score—into that great dormitory that was, in fact, nothing but one long attic or grange beneath the bare roof. And sometimes the maids told tales or slept soon, and sometimes their gallants, grooms and others, came climbing through the windows with rope ladders. They would bring pasties and wines and lights, and coarsely they would revel.

"Why," she said, "I had a gallant myself. He was a musician, but I have forgot his name. Aye, and then there was another, Dearham, I think; but I have heard he is since dead. He may have been my cousin; we were so many in family, I have a little forgot."

She stood still, searching her memory, with her eyes distant. The Lady Mary surveyed her face with a curious irony.

"Why, what a simple Queen you are!" she said. "This is something rustic."

The Queen joined her hands together before her, as if she caught at a clue.

"I do remember me," she said. "It was a make of a comedy. This Dearham, calling himself my cousin, beat this music musician for calling himself my gallant. Then goes the musicker to my grandam, bidding the old Duchess rise up again one hour after she had sought her bed. So comes my grandam and turns the key in the padlock and looketh in over all the gallimaufrey of lights and pasties and revels."

"Why," she continued. "I think I was beaten upon that occasion, but I could not well tell why. And I was put to sleep in another room. And later came my father home from some war. And he was angry that I had consorted so with false minions, and had me away to his own poor house. And there I had Udal for my Magister and evil fare and many beatings. But this Mary Lascelles was my bed-fellow."

"Why, forget it," the Lady Mary said again.

"Other teachers would bid me remember it that I might remain humble," Katharine answered.

"Y'are humble enow and to spare," the Lady Mary said. "And these are not good memories for such a place as this. Y'had best keep this Mary Lascelles at a great distance."

Katharine said—

"No; for I have passed my word."

"Then reward her very fully," the Lady Mary commended, and the Queen answered—

"No, for that is against my conscience. What have I to fear now that I be Queen?"

Mary shrugged her squared shoulders.

"Where is your Latin," she said, "with its *nulla dies felix*—call no day fortunate till it be ended."

"I will set another text against that," she said, "and that from holy sayings—that *justus ab aestimatione non timebit*."

"Well," Mary answered, "you will make your bed how you will. But I think you would better have learned of these maids how to steer a course than of your Magister and the Signor Plutarchus."

The Queen did not answer her, save by begging her to read the King's letter to his Holiness.

"And surely," she said, "if I had never read in the noble Romans I had never had the trick of tongue to gar the King do so much of what I will."

"Why, God help you," her step-daughter said. "Pray you may never come to repent it."

PART II
THE THREATENED RIFT

I

In these summer days there was much faring abroad in the broad lands to north and to south of the Pontefract Castle. The sunlight lay across moors and uplands. The King was come with all his many to Newcastle; but no Scots King was there to meet him. So he went farther to northwards. His butchers drove before him herds of cattle that they slew some of each night: their hooves made a broad and beaten way before the King's horses. Behind came an army of tent men: cooks, servers, and sutlers. For, since they went where new castles were few, at times they must sleep on moorsides, and they had tents all of gold cloth and black, with gilded tent-poles and cords of silk and silver wire. The lords and principal men of those parts came out to meet him with green boughs, and music, and slain deer, and fair wooden kegs filled with milk. But when he was come near to Berwick there was still no Scots King to meet him, and it became manifest that the King's nephew would fail that tryst. Henry, riding among his people, swore a mighty oath that he would take way even into Edinburgh town and there act as he listed, for he had with him nigh on seven thousand men of all arms and some cannon which he had been minded to display for the instruction of his nephew. But he had, in real truth, little stomach for this feat. For, if he would go into Scotland armed, he must wait till he got together all the men that the Council of the North had under arms. These were scattered over the whole of the Border country, and it must be many days before he had them all there together. And already the summer was well advanced, and if he delayed much longer his return, the after progress from Pontefract to London must draw them to late in the winter. And he was little minded that either Katharine or his son should bear the winter travel. Indeed, he sent a messenger back to Pontefract with orders that the Prince should be sent forthwith with a great guard to Hampton Court, so that he should reach that place before the nights grew cold.

And, having stayed in camp four days near the Scots border—for he loved well to live in a tent, since it re-awoke in him the ardour of his youth and made him think himself not so old a man—he delivered over to the Earl Marshal forty Scots borderers and cattle thieves that had been taken that summer. These men he had meant to have handed, pardoned, to the Scots King when he met him. But the Earl Marshal set up, along the road into Scotland, from where the stone marks the border, a row of forty gallows, all high, but some higher than others; for some of the prisoners were men of condition. And, within sight of a waiting crowd of Scots that had come down to the boundaries of their land to view the King of England, Norfolk hanged on these trees the forty men.

And, laughing over their shoulders at this fine harvest of fruit, gibbering and dangling against the heavens on high, the King and his host rode back into the Border country. It was pleasant to ride in the summer weather, and they hunted and rendered justice by the way, and heard tales of battle that there had been before in the north country.

But there was one man, Thomas Culpepper, in the town of Edinburgh to whom this return was grievous. He had been in these outlandish parts now for more than nineteen months. The Scots were odious to him, the town was odious; he had no stomach for his food, and such clothes as he had were ragged, for he would wear nothing that had there been woven. He was even a sort of prisoner. For he had been appointed to wait on the King's Ambassador to the King of Scots, and the last thing that Throckmorton, the notable spy, had done before he had left the Court had been to write to Edinburgh that T. Culpepper, the Queen's cousin, who was a dangerous man, was to be kept very close and given no leave of absence.

And one thing very much had aided this: for, upon receiving news, or the rumour of news, that his cousin Katharine Howard—he was her mother's brother's son—had wedded the King, or had been shown for Queen at Hampton Court, he had suddenly become seized with such a rage that, incontinently, he had run his sword through an old fishwife in the fishmarket where he was who had given him the news, newly come by sea, thinking that because he was an Englishman this marriage of his King might gladden him. The fishwife died among her fish, and Culpepper with his sword fell upon all that were near him in the market, till, his heel slipping upon a haddock, he fell, and was fallen upon by a great many men.

He must stay in jail for this till he had compounded with the old woman's heirs and had paid for a great many cuts and bruises. And Sir Nicholas Hoby, happening to be in Edinburgh at that time, understood well what ailed Thomas Culpepper, and that he was mad for love of the Queen his cousin—for was it not this Culpepper that had brought her to the court, and, as it was said, had aforetime sold farms to buy her food and gowns when, her father being a poor man, she was well-nigh starving? Therefore Sir Nicholas begged alike the Ambassador and the King of Scots that they would keep this madman clapped up till they were very certain that the fit was off him. And, what with the charges of blood ransom and jailing for nine months, Culpepper had no money at all when at last he was enlarged, but must eat his meals at the Ambassador's table, so that he could not in any way come away into England till he had written for more money and had earned a further salary. And that again was a matter of many months, and later he spent more in drinking and with Scots women till he persuaded himself that he had forgotten his cousin that was now a Queen. Moreover, it was made clear to him by those about him that it was death to leave his post unpermitted.

But, with the coming of the Court up into the north parts, his impatience grew again, so that he could no longer eat but only drink and fight. It was rumoured that the Queen was riding with the King, and he swore a mighty oath that he would beg of her or of the King leave at last to be gone from that hateful city; and the nearer came the King the more his ardour grew. So that, when the news came that the King was turned back, Culpepper could no longer compound it with himself. He had then a plenty of money, having kept his room for seven days, and the night before that he had won half a barony at dice from a Scots archer. But he had no passport into England; therefore, because he was afraid to ask for one, being certain of a refusal, he blacked his face and hands with coal and then took refuge on a coble, leaving the port of Leith for Durham. He had well bribed the master of this ship to take him as one of his crew. In Durham he stayed neither to wash nor to eat, but, having bought himself a horse, he rode after the King's progress that was then two days' journey to the south, and came up with them. He had no wits left more than to ask of the sutlers at the tail of the host where the Queen was. They laughed at this apparition upon a haggard horse, and one of them that was a notable cutpurse took all the gold that he had, only giving him in exchange the news that the Queen was at Pontefract, from which place she had never stirred. With a little silver that he had in another bag he bought himself a provision of food, a store of drink, and a poor Kern to guide him, running at his saddle-bow.

He saw neither hills nor valleys, neither heather nor ling: he had no thoughts but only that of finding the Queen his cousin. At times the tears ran down his begrimed face, at times he waved his sword in the air and, spurring his horse, he swore great oaths. How he fared, where he rested, by what roads he went over the hills, that he never knew. Without a doubt the Kern guided him faithfully.

For the Queen, having news that the King was nearly come within a day's journey, rode out towards the north to meet him. And as she went along the road, she saw, upon a hillside not very far away, a man that sat upon a dead horse, beating it and tugging at its bridle. Beside him stood a countryman, in a garment of furs and pelts, with rawhide boots. She had a great many men and ladies riding behind her, and she had come as far as she was minded to go. So she reined in her horse and sent two prickers to ask who these men were.

And when she heard that this was a traveller, robbed of all his money and insensate, and his poor guide who knew nothing of who he might be, she turned her cavalcade back and commanded that the traveller should be borne to the castle on a litter of boughs and there attended to and comforted until again he could take the road. And she made occasion upon this to comment how ill it was for travellers that the old monasteries were done away with. For in the old time there were seven monasteries between there and Durham, wherein poor travellers might lodge. Then, if a merchant were robbed upon the highways, he could be housed at convenient stages on his road home, and might afterwards send recompense to the good fathers or not as he pleased or was able. Now, there was no harbourage left on all that long road, and, but for the grace of God, that pitiful traveller might have lain there till the ravens picked out his eyes.

And some commended the Queen's words and actions, and some few, behind their hands, laughed at her for her soft heart. And the more Lutheran sort said that it was God's mercy that the old monasteries were gone; for they had, they said, been the nests for lowsels, idle wayfarers, palmers, pilgrims, and the like. And, praise God, since that clearance fourteen thousand of these had been hanged by the waysides for sturdy rogues, to the great purging of the land.

II

In the part of Lincolnshire that is a little to the northeastward of Stamford was a tract of country that had been granted to the monks of St Radigund's at Dover by William the Conqueror. These monks had drained this land many centuries before, leaving the superintendence of the work at first to priors by them appointed, and afterwards, when the dykes, ditches, and flood walls were all made, to knights and poor gentlemen, their tenants, who farmed the land and kept up the defences against inundations, paying scot and lot to a bailiff and water-wardens and jurats, just as was done on the Romney marshes by the bailiff and jurats of that level.

And one of these tenants, holding two hundred acres in a simple fee from St Radigund's for a hundred and fifty years back, had been always a man of the name of Hall. It was an Edward Hall that Mary Lascelles had married when she was a maid at the Duchess of Norfolk's. This Edward Hall was then a squire, a little above the condition of a groom, in the Duchess's service. His parents dwelled still on the farm which was called Neot's End, because it was in the angle of the great dyke called St Neot's and the little sewer where St Radigund's land had its boundary stone.

But in the troublesome days of the late Privy Seal, Edward Hall had informed Throckmorton the spy of a conspiracy and rising that was hatching amongst the Radigund's men a little before the Pilgrimage of Grace, when all the north parts rose. For the Radigund's men cried out and murmured amongst themselves that if the Priory was done away with there would be an end of their easy and comfortable tenancy. Their rents had been estimated and appointed a great number of years before, when all goods and the produce of the earth were very low priced. And the tenants said that if now the King took their lands to himself or gave them to some great lord, very heavy burdens would be laid upon them and exacted; whereas in some years under easy priors the monks forgot their distant territory, and in bad seasons they took no rents at all. And even under hard and exacting priors the monks could take no more than their rentals, which were so small. They said, too, that the King and Thomas Cromwell would make them into heathen Greeks and turn their children to be Saracens. So these Radigund's men meditated a rising and conspiracy.

But, because Edward Hall informed Throckmorton of what was agate, a posse was sent into that country, and most of the men were hanged and their lands all taken from them. Those that survived from the jailing betook themselves to the road, and became sturdy beggars, so that many of them too came to the gallows tree.

Most of the land was granted to the Sieur Throckmorton with the abbey's buildings and tithe barns. But the Halls' farm and another of near three hundred acres were granted to Edward Hall. Then it was that Edward Hall could marry and take his wife, Mary Lascelles, down into Lincolnshire to Neot's End. But when the Pilgrimage of Grace came, and the great risings all over Lincolnshire, very early the rioters came to Neot's End, and they burned the farm and the byres, they killed all the beasts or drove them off, they trampled down the corn and laid waste the flax fields. And, between two willow trees along the great dyke, they set a pole, and from it they hanged Edward Hall over the waters, so that he dried and was cured like a ham in the smoke from his own stacks.

Then Mary Lascelles' case was a very miserable one; for she had to fend for the aged father and bedridden mother of Edward Hall, and there were no beasts left but only a few geese and ducks that the rebels could not lay their hands on. And the only home that they had was the farmhouse that was upon Edward Hall's other farm, and that they had let fall nearly into ruin. And for a long time no men would work for her.

But at last, after the rebellion was pitifully ended, a few hinds came to her, and she made a shift. And it was better still after Privy Seal fell, for then came Throckmorton the spy into his lands, and he brought with him carpenters and masons and joiners to make his house fair, and some of these men he lent to Mary Hall. But it had been prophesied by a wise woman in those parts that no land that had been taken from the monks would prosper. And, because all the jurats, bailiffs, and water-wardens had been hanged either on the one part or the other and no more had been appointed, at about that time the sewers began to clog up, the lands to swamp, murrain and fluke to strike the beasts and the sheep, and night mists to blight the grain and the fruit blossoms. So that even Throckmorton had little good of his wealth and lands.

Thus one morning to Mary Hall, who stood before her door feeding her geese and ducks, there came a little boy running to say that men-at-arms stood on the other side of the dyke that was very swollen and grey and broad. And they shouted that they came from the Queen's Highness, and would have a boat sent to ferry them over.

The colour came into Mary Hall's pale face, for even there she had heard that her former bedfellow was come to be Queen. And at times even she had thought to write to the Queen to help her in her misery. But always she had been afraid, because she thought that the Queen might remember her only as one that had wronged her childish innocence. For she remembered that the maids' dormitory at the old Duchess's had been no cloister of pure nuns. So that, at best, she was afraid, and she sent her yard-worker and a shepherd a great way round to fetch the larger boat of two to ferry over the Queen's men. Then she went indoors to redd up the houseplace and to attire herself.

To the old farmstead, that was made of wood hung over here and there with tilework with a base of bricks, she had added a houseplace for the old folk to sit all day. It was built of wattles that had had clay cast over them, and was whitened on the outside and thatched nearly down to the ground like any squatter's hut; it had cupboards of wood nearly all round it, and beneath the cupboards were lockers worn smooth with men sitting upon them, after the Dutch fashion—for there in Lincolnshire they had much traffic with the Dutch. There was a great table made of one slab of a huge oak from near Boston. Here they all ate. And above the ingle was another slab of oak from the same tree. Her little old step-mother sat in a stuff chair covered with a sheep-skin; she sat there night and day, shivering with the shaking palsy. At times she let out of her an eldritch shriek, very like the call of a hedgehog; but she never spoke, and she was fed with a spoon by a little misbegotten son of Edward Hall's. The old step-father sat always opposite her; he had no use of his legs, and his head was always stiffly screwed round towards the door as if he were peering, but that was the rheumatism. To atone for his wife's dumbness, he chattered incessantly whenever anyone was on that floor; but because he spoke always in Lincolnshire, Mary Hall could scarce understand him, and indeed she had long ceased to listen. He spoke of forgotten floods and ploughings, ancient fairs, the boundaries of fields long since flooded over, of a visit to Boston that King Edward IV had made, and of how he, for his fair speech and old lineage, had been chosen of all the Radigund's men to present into the King's hands three silver horseshoes. Behind his back was a great dresser with railed shelves, having upon them a little pewter ware and many wooden bowls for the hinds' feeding. A door on the right side, painted black, went down into the cellar beneath the old house. Another door, of bars of iron with huge locks from the old monastery, went into the old house where slept the maids and the hinds. This was always open by day but locked in the dark hours. For the hinds were accounted brutish lumps that went savage at night, like wild beasts, so that, if they spared the master's throat, which was unlikely, it was certain that they would little spare the salted meat, the dried fish, the mead, metheglin, and cyder that their poor cellar afforded. The floor was of stamped clay, wet and sweating but covered with rushes, so that the place had a mouldering smell. Behind the heavy door there were huge bolts and crossbars against robbers: the raftered ceiling was so low that it touched her hair when she walked across the floor. The windows had no glass but were filled with a thin reddish sheep-skin like parchment. Before the stairway was a wicket gate to keep the dogs—of whom there were many, large and fierce, to protect them alike from robbers and the hinds—to keep the dogs from going into the upper room.

Each time that Mary Hall came into this home of hers her heart sank lower; for each day the corner posts gave sideways a little more, the cupboard bulged, the doors were loth to close or open. And more and more the fields outside were inundated, the lands grew sour, the sheep would not eat or died of the fluke.

"And surely," she would cry out at times, "God created me for other guesswork than this!"

At nights she was afraid, and shivered at the thought of the fens and the black and trackless worlds all round her; and the ravens croaked, night-hawks screamed, the dog-foxes cried out, and the flames danced over the swampy grounds. Her mirror was broken on the night that they hanged her husband: she had never had another but the water in her buckets, so that she could not tell whether she had much aged or whether she were still brown-haired and pink-cheeked, and she had forgotten how to laugh, and was sure that there were crow's-feet about her eyelids.

Her best gown was all damp and mouldy in the attic that was her bower. She made it meet as best she could, and indeed she had had so little fat living, sitting at the head of her table with a whip for unruly hinds and louts before her—so little fat living that she could well get into her wedding-gown of yellow cramosyn. She smoothed her hair back into her cord hood that for so long had not come out of its press. She washed her face in a bucket of water: that and the press and her bed with grey woollen curtains were all the furnishing her room had. The

FORD MADOX FORD

straw of the roof caught in her hood when she moved, and she heard her old father-in-law cackling to the serving-maids through the cracks of the floor.

When she came down there were approaching, across the field before the door, six men in scarlet and one in black, having all the six halberds and swords, and one a little banner, but the man in black had a sword only. Their horses were tethered in a clump on the farther side of the dyke. Within the room the serving-maids were throwing knives and pewter dishes with a great din on to the table slab. They dropped drinking-horns and the salt-cellar itself all of a heap into the rushes. The grandfather was cackling from his chair; a hen and its chickens ran screaming between the maids' feet. Then Lascelles came in at the doorway.

III

The Sieur Lascelles looked round him in that dim cave.

"Ho!" he said, "this place stinks," and he pulled from his pocket a dried and shrivelled orange-peel purse stuffed with cloves and ginger. "Ho!" he said to the cornet that was come behind him with the Queen's horsemen. "Come not in here. This will breed a plague amongst your men!" and he added—

"Did I not tell you my sister was ill-housed?"

"Well, I was not prepared against this," the cornet said. He was a man with a grizzling beard that had little patience away from the Court, where he had a bottle that he loved and a crony or two that he played all day at chequers with, except when the Queen rode out; then he was of her train. He did not come over the sill, but spoke sharply to his men.

"Ungird not here," he said. "We will go farther." For some of them were for setting their pikes against the mud wall and casting their swords and heavy bottle-belts on to the table before the door. The old man in the armchair began suddenly to prattle to them all—of a horse-thief that had been dismembered and then hanged in pieces thirty years before. The cornet looked at him for a moment and said—

"Sir, you are this woman's father-in-law, I do think. Have you aught to report against her?" He bent in at the door, holding his nose. The old man babbled of one Pease-Cod Noll that had no history to speak of but a swivel eye.

"Well," the grizzled cornet said, "I shall get little sense here." He turned upon Mary Hall.

"Mistress," he said, "I have a letter here from the Queen's High Grace," and, whilst he fumbled in his belt to find a little wallet that held the letter, he spoke on: "But I misdoubt you cannot read. Therefore I shall tell you the Queen's High Grace commandeth you to come into her service—or not, as the report of your character shall be. But at any rate you shall come to the castle."

Mary Hall could find no words for men of condition, so long she had been out of the places where such are found. She swallowed in her throat and held her breast over her heart.

"Where is the village here?" the cornet said, "or what justice is there that can write you a character under his seal?"

She made out to say that there was no village, all the neighbourhood

FORD MADOX FORD

having been hanged. A half-mile from there there was the house of Sir Nicholas Throckmorton, a justice. From the house-end he might see it, or he might have a hind to guide him. But he would have no guide; he would have no man nor maid nor child to go from there to the justice's house. He set one soldier to guard the back door and one the front, that none came out nor went beyond the dyke-end.

"Neither shall you go, Sir Lascelles," he said.

"Well, give me leave with my sister to walk this knoll," Lascelles said good-humouredly. "We shall not corrupt the grass blades to bear false witness of my sister's chastity."

"Ay, you may walk upon this mound," the cornet answered. Having got out the packet of the Queen's letter, he girded up his belt again.

"You will get you ready to ride with me," he said to Mary Hall. "For I will not be in these marshes after nightfall, but will sleep at Shrimpton Inn."

He looked around him and added—

"I will have three of your geese to take with us," he said. "Kill me them presently."

Lascelles looked after him as he strode away round the house with the long paces of a stiff horseman.

"Before God," he laughed, "that is one way to have information about a quean. Now are we prisoners whilst he inquires after your character."

"Oh, alack!" Mary Hall said, and she cast up her hands.

"Well, we are prisoners till he come again," her brother said good-humouredly. "But this is a foul hole. Come out into the sunlight."

She said—

"If you are with them, they cannot come to take me prisoner."

He looked her full in the eyes with his own that twinkled inscrutably. He said very slowly—

"Were your mar-locks and prinking-prankings so very evil at the old Duchess's?"

She grew white: she shrank away as if he had threatened her with his fist.

"The Queen's Highness was such a child," she said. "She cannot remember. I have lived very godly since."

"I will do what I can to save you," he said. "Let me hear about it, as, being prisoners, we may never come off."

"You!" she cried out. "You who stole my wedding portion!"

He laughed deviously.

"Why, I have laid it up so well for you that you may wed a knight now if you do my bidding. I was ever against your wedding Hall."

"You lie!" she said. "You gar'd me do it."

The maids were peeping out of the cellar, whither they had fled.

"Come upon the grass," he said. "I will not be heard to say more than this: that you and I stand and fall together like good sister and goodly brother."

Their faces differed only in that hers was afraid and his smiling as he thought of new lies to tell her. Her face in her hood, pale beneath its weathering, approached the colour of his that shewed the pink and white of indoors. She came very slowly near him, for she was dazed. But when she was almost at the sill he caught her hand and drew it beneath his elbow.

"Tell me truly," she said, "shall I see the Court or a prison? . . . But you cannot speak truth, nor ever could when we were tiny twins. God help me: last Sunday I had the mind to wed my yard-man. I would become such a liar as thou to come away from here."

"Sister," he said, "this I tell you most truly: that this shall fall out according as you obey me and inform me"; and, because he was a little the taller, he leaned over her as they walked away together.

ON THE FOURTH DAY FROM then they were come to the great wood that is to south and east of the castle of Pontefract. Here Lascelles, who had ridden much with his sister, forsook her and went ahead of the slow and heavy horses of that troop of men. The road was broadened out to forty yards of green turf between the trees, for this was a precaution against ambushes of robbers. Across the road, after he had ridden alone for an hour and a half, there was a guard of four men placed. And here, whilst he searched for his pass to come within the limits of the Court, he asked what news, and where the King was.

It was told him that the King lay still at the Fivefold Vents, two days' progress from the castle, and as it chanced that a verderer's pricker came out of the wood where he had been to mark where the deer lay for tomorrow's killing, Lascelles bade this man come along with him for a guide.

"Sir, ye cannot miss the way," the pricker said surlily. "I have my deer to watch."

"I will have you to guide me," Lascelles said, "for I little know these parts."

"Well," the pricker answered him, "it is true that I have not often seen you ride a-hawking."

Whilst they went along the straight road, Lascelles, who unloosened the woodman's tongue with a great drink of sherry-sack, learned that it was said that only very unwillingly did the King lie so long at the Fivefold Vents. For on the morrow there was to be driven by, up there, a great herd of moor stags and maybe a wolf or two. The King would home with his wife, it was reported, but the younger lords had been so importunate with him to stay and abide this gallant chase and great slaughter that, they having ridden loyally with him, he had yielded to their prayers and stayed there—twenty-four hours, it was said.

"Why, you know a great deal," Lascelles answered.

"We who stand and wait have needs have knowledge," the woodman said, "for we have little else."

"Aye, 'tis a hard service," Lascelles said. "Did you see the Queen's Highness o' Thursday week borrow a handkerchief of Sir Roger Pelham to lure her falcon back?"

"That did not I," the woodman answered, "for o' Thursday week it was a frost and the Queen rode not out."

"Well, it was o' Saturday," Lascelles said.

"Nor was it yet o' Saturday," the woodman cried; "I will swear it. For o' Saturday the Queen's Highness shot with the bow, and Sir Roger Pelham, as all men know, fell with his horse on Friday, and lies up still."

"Then it was Sir Nicholas Rochford," Lascelles persisted.

"Sir," the woodman said, "you have a very wrong tale, and patent it is that little you ride a-hunting."

"Well, I mind my book," Lascelles said. "But wherefore?"

"Sir," the woodman answered, "it is thus: The Queen when she rides a-hawking has always behind her her page Toussaint, a little boy. And this little boy holdeth ever the separate lures for each hawk that the Queen setteth up. And the falcon or hawk or genette or tiercel having stooped, the Queen will call upon that eyass for the lure appropriated to each bird as it chances. And very carefully the Queen's Highness observeth the laws of the chase, of venery and hawking. For the which I honour her."

Lascelles said, "Well, well!"

"As for the borrowing of a handkerchief," the woodman pursued, "that is a very idle tale. For, let me tell you, a lady might borrow a jewelled feather or a scarlet pouch or what not that is bright and shall take a bird's eye—a little mirror upon a cord were a good thing. But a handkerchief! Why, Sir Bookman, that a lady can only do if she will signify to all the world: 'This knight is my servant and I his mistress.' Those very words it signifieth—and that the better for it showeth that that lady is minded to let her hawk go, luring the gentleman to her with that favour of his."

"Well, well," Lascelles said, "I am not so ignorant that I did not know that. Therefore I asked you, for it seemed a very strange thing."

"It is a very foolish tale and very evil," the man answered. "For this I will swear: that the Queen's Highness—and I and her honour for it—observeth very jealously the laws of wood and moorland and chase."

"So I have heard," Lascelles said. "But I see the castle. I will not take you farther, but will let you go back to the goodly deer."

"Pray God they be not wandered fore," the woodman said. "You could have found this way without me."

THERE WAS BUT ONE ROAD into the castle, and that from the south, up a steep green bank. Up the roadway Lascelles must ride his horse past four men that bore a litter made of two pikes wattled with green boughs and covered with a horse-cloth. As Lascelles passed by the very head of it, the man that lay there sprang off it to his feet, and cried out—

"I be the Queen's cousin and servant. I brought her to the Court." Lascelles' horse sprang sideways, a great bound up the bank. He galloped ten paces ahead before the rider could stay him and turn round. The man, all rags and with a black face, had fallen into the dust of the road, and still cried out outrageously. The bearers set down the litter, wiped their brows, and then, falling all four upon Culpepper, made to carry him by his legs and arms, for they were weary of laying him upon the litter from which incessantly he sprang.

But before them upon his horse was Lascelles and impeded their way. Culpepper drew in and pushed out his legs and arms, so that they all four staggered, and—

"For God's sake, master," one of them grunted out, "stand aside that we may pass. We have toil enow in bearing him."

"Why, set the poor gentleman down upon the litter," Lascelles said, "and let us talk a little."

The men set Culpepper on the horse-cloth, and one of them knelt down to hold him there.

"If you will lend us your horse to lay him across, we may come more easily up," one said. In these days the position and trade of a spy was so little esteemed—it had been far other with the great informers of Privy Seal's day—that these men, being of the Queen's guard, would talk roughly to Lascelles, who was a mere poor gentleman of the Archbishop's if his other vocation could be neglected. Lascelles sat, his hand upon his chin.

"You use him very roughly if this be the Queen's cousin," he said.

The bearer set back his beard and laughed at the sky.

"This is a coif—a poor rag of a merchant," he cried out. "If this were the Queen's cousin should we bear him thus on a clout?"

"I am the Queen's cousin, T. Culpepper," Culpepper shouted at the sky. "Who be you that stay me from her?"

"Why, you may hear plainly," the bearer said. "He is mazed, doited, starved, thirsted, and a seer of visions."

Lascelles pondered, his elbow upon his saddle-peak, his chin caught in his hand.

"How came ye by him?" he asked.

One with another they told him the tale, how, the Queen being ridden towards the north parts, at the extreme end of her ride had seen the man, at a distance, among the heather, flogging a dead horse with a moorland kern beside him. He was a robbed, parched, fevered, and amazed traveller. The Queen's Highness, compassionating, had bidden bear him to the castle and comfort and cure him, not having looked upon his face or heard his tongue. For, for sure then, she had let him die where he was; since, no sooner were these four, his new bearers, nearly come up among the knee-deep heather, than this man had started up, his eyes upon the Queen's cavalcade and many at a distance. And, with his sword drawn and screaming, he had cried out that, if that was the Queen, he was the Queen's cousin. They had tripped up his heels in a bed of ling and quieted him with a clout on the poll from an axe end.

"But now we have him here," the eldest said; "where we shall bestow him we know not."

Lascelles had his eyes upon the sick man's face as if it fascinated him, and, slowly, he got down from his horse. Culpepper then lay very still with his eyes closed, but his breast heaved as though against tight and strong ropes that bound him.

"I think I do know this gentleman for one John Robb," he said. "Are you very certain the Queen's Highness did not know his face?"

"Why, she came not ever within a quarter mile of him," the bearer said.

"Then it is a great charity of the Queen to show mercy to a man she hath never seen," Lascelles answered absently. He was closely casting his eyes over Culpepper. Culpepper lay very still, his begrimed face to the sky, his hands abroad above his head. But when Lascelles bent over him it was as if he shuddered, and then he wept.

Lascelles bent down, his hands upon his knees. He was afraid—he was very afraid. Thomas Culpepper, the Queen's cousin, he had never seen in his life. But he had heard it reported that he had red hair and beard, and went always dressed in green with stockings of red. And this man's hair was red, and his beard, beneath coal grime, was a curly red, and his coat, beneath a crust of black filth, was Lincoln green and of a good cloth. And, beneath the black, his stockings were of red silk. He reflected slowly, whilst the bearers laughed amongst themselves at this Queen's kinsman in rags and filth.

Lascelles gave them his bottle of sack to drink empty among them, that he might have the longer time to think.

If this were indeed the Queen's cousin, come unknown to the Queen and mazed and muddled in himself to Pontefract, what might not Lascelles make of him? For all the world knew that he loved her with a mad love—he had sold farms to buy her gowns. It was he that had brought her to Court, upon an ass, at Greenwich, when her mule—as all men knew—had stumbled upon the threshold. Once before, it was said, Culpepper had burst in with his sword drawn upon the King and Kate Howard when they sat together. And Lascelles trembled with eagerness at the thought of what use he might not make of this mad and insolent lover of the Queen's!

But did he dare?

Culpepper had been sent into Scotland to secure him up, away at the farthest limits of the realm. Then, if he was come back? This grime was the grime of a sea-coal ship! He knew that men without passports, outlaws and the like, escaped from Scotland on the Durham ships that went to Leith with coal. And this man came on the Durham road. Then. . .

If it were Culpepper he had come unpermitted. He was an outlaw. Dare Lascelles have trade with—dare he harbour—an outlaw? It would be unbeknown to the Queen's Highness! He kicked his heels with impatience to come to a resolution.

He reflected swiftly:

What hitherto he had were: some tales spread abroad about the Queen's lewd Court—tales in London Town. He had, too, the keeper of the Queen's door bribed and talked into his service and interest. And he had his sister. . .

His sister would, with threatening, tell tales of the Queen before marriage. And she would find him other maids and grooms, some no doubt more willing still than Mary Hall. But the keeper of the Queen's door! And, in addition, the Queen's cousin mad of love for her! What might he not do with these two?

The prickly sweat came to his forehead. Four horsemen were issuing from the gate of the castle above. He must come to a decision. His fingers trembled as if they were a pickpocket's near a purse of gold.

He straightened his back and stood erect.

"Yes," he said very calmly, "this is my friend John Robb."

He added that this man had been in Edinburgh where the Queen's cousin was. He had had letters from him that told how they were sib and rib. Thus this fancy had doubtless come into his brain at sight of the Queen in his madness.

He breathed calmly, having got out these words, for now the doubt was ended. He would have both the Queen's door-keeper and the Queen's mad lover.

He bade the bearers set Culpepper upon his horse and, supporting him, lead him to a room that he would hire of the Archbishop's chamberlain, near his own in the dark entrails of the castle. And there John Robb should live at his expenses.

And when the men protested that, though this was very Christian of Lascelles, yet they would have recompense of the Queen for their toils, he said that he himself would give them a crown apiece, and they might get in addition what recompense from the Queen's steward that they could. He asked them each their names and wrote them down, pretending that it was that he might send each man his crown piece.

So, when the four horsemen were ridden past, the men hoisted Culpepper into Lascelles' horse and went all together up into the castle.

But, that night, when Culpepper lay in a stupor, Lascelles went to the Archbishop's chamberlain and begged that four men, whose names he had written down, might be chosen to go in the Archbishop's paritor's guard that went next dawn to Ireland over the sea to bring back tithes from Dublin. And, next day, he had Culpepper moved to another room; and, in three days' time, he set it about in the castle that the Queen's cousin was come from Scotland. By that time most of the liquor had come down out of Culpepper's brain, but he was still muddled and raved at times.

IV

On that third night the Queen was with the Lady Mary, once more in her chamber, having come down as before, from the chapel in the roof, to pray her submit to her father's will. Mary had withstood her with a more good-humoured irony; and, whilst she was in the midst of her pleadings, a letter marked most pressing was brought to her. The Queen opened it, and raised her eyebrows; she looked down at the subscription and frowned. Then she cast it upon the table.

"Shall there never be an end of old things?" she said.

"Even what old things?" the Lady Mary asked.

The Queen shrugged her shoulders.

"It was not they I came to talk of," she said. "I would sleep early, for the King comes tomorrow and I have much to plead with you."

"I am weary of your pleadings," the Lady Mary said. "You have pleaded enow. If you would be fresh for the King, be first fresh for me. Start a new hare."

The Queen would have gainsaid her.

"I have said you have pleaded enow," the Lady Mary said. "And you have pleaded enow. This no more amuses me. I will wager I guess from whom your letter was."

Reluctantly the Queen held her peace; that day she had read in many ancient books, as well profane as of the Fathers of the Church, and she had many things to say, and they were near her lips and warm in her heart. She was much minded to have good news to give the King against his coming on the morrow; the great good news that should set up in that realm once more abbeys and chapters and the love of God. But she could not press these sayings upon the girl, though she pleaded still with her blue eyes.

"Your letter is from Sir Nicholas Throckmorton," the Lady Mary said. "Even let me read it."

"You did know that that knight was come to Court again?" the Queen said.

"Aye; and that you would not see him, but like a fool did bid him depart again."

"You will ever be calling me a fool," Katharine retorted, "for giving ear to my conscience and hating spies and the suborners of false evidence."

"Why," the Lady Mary answered, "I do call it a folly to refuse to give ear to the tale of a man who has ridden far and fast, and at the risk of a penalty to tell it you."

"Why," Katharine said, "if I did forbid his coming to the Court under a penalty, it was because I would not have him here."

"Yet he much loved you, and did you some service."

"He did me a service of lies," the Queen said, and she was angry. "I would not have had him serve me. By his false witness Cromwell was cast down to make way for me. But I had rather have cast down Cromwell by the truth which is from God. Or I had rather he had never been cast down. And that I swear."

"Well, you are a fool," the Lady Mary said. "Let me look upon this knight's letter."

"I have not read it," Katharine said.

"Then will I," the Lady Mary answered. She made across the room to where the paper lay upon the table beside the great globe of the earth. She came back; she turned her round to the Queen; she made her a deep reverence, so that her black gown spread out stiffly around her, and, keeping her eyes ironically on Katharine's face, she mounted backward up to the chair that was beneath the dais.

Katharine put her hand over her heart.

"What mean you?" she said. "You have never sat there before."

"That is not true," the Lady Mary said harshly. "For this last three days I have practised how, thus backward, I might climb to this chair and, thus seemly, sit in it."

"Even then?" Katharine asked.

"Even then I will be asked no more questions," her step-daughter answered. "This signifieth that I ha' heard enow o' thy voice, Queen."

Katharine did not dare to speak, for she knew well this girl's tyrannous and capricious nature. But she was nearly faint with emotion and reached sideways for the chair at the table; there she sat and gazed at the girl beneath the dais, her lips parted, her body leaning forward.

Mary spread out the great sheet of Throckmorton's parchment letter upon her black knees. She bent forward so that the light from the mantel at the room-end might fall upon the writing.

"It seemeth," she said ironically, "that one descrieth better at the humble end of the room than here on high"—and she read whilst the Queen panted.

At last she raised her eyes and bent them darkly upon the Queen's face.

"Will you do what this knight asks?" she uttered. "For what he asks seemeth prudent."

"A' God's name," Katharine said, "let me not now hear of this man."

"Why," the Lady Mary answered coolly, "if I am to be of the Queen's alliance I must be of the Queen's council and my voice have a weight."

"But will you? Will you?" Katharine brought out.

"Will you listen to my voice?" Mary said. "I will not listen to yours. Hear now what this goodly knight saith. For, if I am to be your well-wisher, I must call him goodly that so well wishes to you."

Katharine wrung her hands.

"Ye torture me," she said.

"Well, I have been tortured," Mary answered, "and I have come through it and live."

She swallowed in her throat, and thus, with her eyes upon the writing, brought out the words—

"This knight bids you beware of one Mary Lascelles or Hall, and her brother, Edward Lascelles, that is of the Archbishop's service."

"I will not hear what Throckmorton says," Katharine answered.

"Ay, but you shall," Mary said, "or I come down from this chair. I am not minded to be allied to a Queen that shall be undone. That is not prudence."

"God help me!" the Queen said.

"God helps most willingly them that take counsel with themselves and prudence," her step-daughter answered; "and these are the words of the knight." She held up the parchment and read out:

"'Therefore I—and you know how much your well-wisher I be— upon my bended knees do pray you do one of two things: either to put out both these twain from your courts and presence, or if that you cannot or will not do, so richly to reward them as that you shall win them to your service. For a little rotten fruit will spread a great stink; a small ferment shall pollute a whole well. And these twain, I am advised, assured, convinced, and have convicted them, will spread such a rotten fog and mist about your reputation and so turn even your good and gracious actions to evil seeming that—I swear and vow, O most high Sovereign, for whom I have risked, as you wot, life, limb and the fell rack—'"

The Lady Mary looked up at the Queen's face.

"Will you not listen to the pleadings of this man?" she said.

"I will so reward Lascelles and his sister as they have merited." the Queen said. "So much and no more. And not all the pleadings of this knight shall move me to listen to any witness that he brings against any man nor maid. So help me, God; for I do know how he served his master Cromwell."

"For love of thee!" the Lady Mary said.

The Queen wrung her hands as if she would wash a stain from them.

"God help me!" she said. "I prayed the King for the life of Privy Seal that was!"

"He would not hear thee," the Lady Mary said. She looked long upon the Queen's face with unmoved and searching eyes.

"It is a new thing to me," she said, "to hear that you prayed for Privy Seal's life."

"Well, I prayed," Katharine said, "for I did not think he worked treason against the King."

The Lady Mary straightened her back where she sat.

"I think I will not show myself less queenly than you," she said. "For I be of a royal race. But hear this knight."

And again she read:

"'I have it from the lips of the cornet that came with this Lascelles to fetch this Mary Lascelles or Hall: I, Throckmorton, a knight, swear that I heard with mine own ears, how for ever as they rode, this Lascelles plied this cornet with questions about your high self. As thus: "Did you favour any gentleman when you rode out, the cornet being of your guard?" or, "Had he heard a tale of one Pelham, a knight, of whom you should have taken a kerchief?"—and this, that and the other, for ever, till the cornet spewed at the hearing of him. Now, gracious and most high Sovereign Consort, what is it that this man seeketh?"'

Again the Lady Mary paused to look at the Queen.

"Why," Katharine said, "so mine enemies will talk of me. I had been the fool you styled me if I had not awaited it. But—" and she drew up her body highly. "My life is such and such shall be that none such arrow shall pierce my corslet."

"God help you," the Lady Mary said. "What has your life to do with it, if you will not cut out the tongues of slanderers?"

She laughed mirthlessly, and added—

"Now this knight concludes—and it is as if he writhed his hands and knelt and whined and kissed your feet—he concludeth with a prayer that you will let him come again to the Court. 'For,' says he, 'I will clean your vessels, serve you at table, scrape the sweat off your horse, or do all that is vilest. But suffer me to come that I may know and report to you what there is whispered in these jail places.'"

Katharine Howard said—

"I had rather borrow Pelham's kerchief."

The Lady Mary dropped the parchment on to the floor at her side.

"I rede you do as this knight wills," she said; "for, amidst the little sticklers of spies that are here, this knight, this emperor of spies, moves as a pillow of shadow. He stalks amongst them as, in the night, the dread and awful lion of Numidia. He shall be to you more a corslet of proof than all the virtue that your life may borrow from the precepts of Diana. We, that are royal and sit in high places, have our feet in such mire."

"Now before God on His throne," Katharine Howard said, "if you be of royal blood, I will teach you a lesson. For hear me—"

"No, I will hear thee no more," the Lady Mary answered; "I will teach thee. For thou art not the only one in this land to be proud. I will show thee such a pride as shall make thee blush."

She stood up and came slowly down the steps of the dais. She squared back her shoulders and folded her hands before her; she erected her head, and her eyes were dark. When she was come to where the Queen sat, she kneeled down.

"I acknowledge thee to be my mother," she said, "that have married the King, my father. I pray you that you do take me by the hand and set me in that seat that you did raise for me. I pray you that you do style me a princess, royal again in this land. And I pray you to lesson me and teach me that which you would have me do as well as that which it befits me to do. Take me by the hand."

"Nay, it is my lord that should do this," the Queen whispered. Before that she had started to her feet; her face had a flush of joy; her eyes shone with her transparent faith. She brushed back a strand of hair from her brow; she folded her hands on her breasts and raised her glance upwards to seek the dwelling-place of Almighty God and the saints in their glorious array.

"It is my lord should do this!" she said again.

"Speak no more words," the Lady Mary said. "I have heard enow of thy pleadings. You have heard me say that."

She continued upon her knees.

"It is thou or none!" she said. "It is thou or none shall witness this my humiliation and my pride. Take me by the hand. My patience will not last for ever."

The Queen set her hand between the girl's. She raised her to her feet.

When the Lady Mary stood high and shadowy, in black, with her white face beneath that dais, she looked down upon the Queen.

"Now, hear me!" she said. "In this I have been humble to you; but I have been most proud. For I have in my veins a greater blood than thine or the King's, my father's. For, inasmuch as Tudor blood is above Howard's, so my mother's, that was royal of Spain, is above Tudor's. And this it is to be royal—"

"I have had you, a Queen, kneel before me. It is royal to receive petitions—more royal still it is to grant them. And in this, further, I am more proud. For, hearing you say that you had prayed the King for Cromwell's life, I thought, this is a virtue-mad Queen. She shall most likely fall!—Prudence biddeth me not to be of her party. But shall I, who am royal, be prudent? Shall I, who am of the house of Aragon, be more afraid than thou, a Howard?"

"I tell you—No! If you will be undone for the sake of virtue, blindly, and like a fool, unknowing the consequences, I, Mary of Aragon and England, will make alliance with thee, knowing that the alliance is dangerous. And, since it is more valiant to go to a doom knowingly than blindfold, so I do show myself more valiant than thou. For well I know—since I saw my mother die—that virtue is a thing profitless, and impracticable in this world. But you—you think it shall set up temporal monarchies and rule peoples. Therefore, what you do you do for profit. I do it for none."

"Now, by the Mother of God," Katharine Howard said, "this is the gladdest day of my life."

"Pray you," Mary said, "get you gone from my sight and hearing, for I endure ill the appearance and sound of joy. And, Queen, again I bid you beware of calling any day fortunate till its close. For, before midnight you may be ruined utterly. I have known more Queens than thou. Thou art the fifth I have known."

She added—

"For the rest, what you will I will do: submission to the King and such cozening as he will ask of me. God keep you, for you stand in need of it."

AT SUPPER THAT NIGHT THERE sat all such knights and lordlings as ate at the King's expense in the great hall that was in the midmost of the castle, looking on to the courtyard. There were not such a many of them, maybe forty; from the keeper of the Queen's records, the Lord d'Espahn, who sat at the table head, down to the lowest of all, the young Poins, who sat far below the salt-cellar. The greater lords of the Queen's household, like the Lord Dacre of the North, did not eat at this common table, or only when the Queen herself there ate, which she did at midday when there was a feast.

Nevertheless, this eating was conducted with gravity, the Lord d'Espahn keeping a vigilant eye down the table, which was laid with a fair white cloth. It cost a man a fine to be drunk before the white meats were eaten—unless, indeed, a man came drunk to the board—and the salt-cellar of state stood a-midmost of the cloth. It was of silver from Holland, and represented a globe of the earth, opened at the top, and supported by knights' bannerets.

The hall was all of stone, with creamy walls, only marked above the iron torch-holds with brandons of soot. A scutcheon of the King's arms was above one end-door, with the Queen's above the other. Over each window were notable deers' antlers, and over each side-door, that let in the servers from the courtyard, was a scutcheon with the arms of a king deceased that had visited the castle. The roof was all gilded and coloured, and showed knaves' faces leering and winking, so that when a man was in drink, and looked upwards with his head on his chair back, these appeared to have life. The hall was called the Dacre Hall, because the Lords Dacre of the North had built it to be an offering to various kings that died whilst it was a-building.

Such knights as had pages had them behind their chairs, holding napkins and ready to fill the horns with wine or beer. From kitchens or from buttery-hatches the servers ran continually across the courtyard and across the tiled floor, for the table was set back against the farther wall, all the knights being on the wall side, since there were not so many, and thus it was easier to come to them. There was a great clatter with the knives going and the feet on the tiles, but little conversing, for in that keen air eating was the principal thing, and in five minutes a boar or a sheep's head would be stripped till the skull alone was shown.

It was in this manner that Thomas Culpepper came into the hall when they were all well set to, without having many eyes upon him. But the Lord d'Espahn was aware, suddenly, of one that stood beside him.

"Gentleman, will you have a seat?" he said. "Tell me your name and estate, that I may appoint you one." He was a grave lord, with a pointed nose, dented at the end, a grey, square beard, and fresh colours on his face. He wore his bonnet because he was the highest there, and because there were currents of air at the openings of the doors.

Thomas Culpepper's face was of a chalky white. Somewhere Lascelles had found for him a suit of green and red stockings. His red beard framed his face, but his lips were pursed.

"Your seat I will have," he said, "for I am the Queen's cousin, T. Culpepper."

The Lord d'Espahn looked down upon his platter.

"You may not have my seat," he said. "But you shall have this seat at my right hand that is empty. It is a very honourable seat, but mine you may not have for it is the Queen's own that I hold, being her vicar here."

"Your seat I will have," Culpepper said.

The Lord d'Espahn was set upon keeping order and quiet in that place more than on any other thing. He looked again down upon his platter, and then he was aware of a voice that whispered in his ear—

"A' God's name, humour him, for he is very mad," and, turning his eyes a little, he saw that it was Lascelles above his chair head.

"Your seat I will have," Culpepper said again. "And this fellow, that tells me he is the most potent lord there is here, shall serve behind my chair."

The Lord d'Espahn took up his knife and fork in one hand and his manchet of bread in the other. He made as if to bow to Culpepper, who pushed him by the shoulder away. Some lordlings saw this and wondered, but in the noise none heard their words. At the foot of the table the squires said that the Lord d'Espahn must have been found out in a treason. Only the young Poins said that that was the Queen's cousin, come from Scotland, withouten leave, for love of the Queen through whom he was sick in the wits. This news ran through the castle by means of servers, cooks, undercooks, scullions, maids, tiring-maids, and maids of honour, more swiftly than it progressed up the table where men had the meats to keep their minds upon.

Culpepper sat, flung back in his chair, his eyes, lacklustre and open, upon the cloth where his hands sprawled out. He said few words— only when the Lord d'Espahn's server carved boar's head for him, he took one piece in his mouth and then threw the plate full into the server's face. This caused great offence amongst the serving-men, for this server was a portly fellow that had served the Lord d'Espahn many years, and had a face like a ram's, so grave it was. Having drunk a little of his wine, Culpepper turned out the rest upon the cloth; his salt he brushed off his plate with his sleeve. That was remembered for long afterwards by many men and women. And it was as if he could not swallow, for he put down neither meat nor drink, but sat, deadly and pale, so that some said that he was rabid. Once he turned his head to ask the Lord d'Espahn—

"If a quean prove forsworn, and turn to a Queen, what should her true love do?"

The Lord d'Espahn never made any answer, but wagged his beard from side to side, and Culpepper repeated his question three separate times. Finally, the platters were raised, and the Lord d'Espahn went away to the sound of trumpets. Many of the lords there came peering round Culpepper to see what sport he might yield. Lascelles went away, following the scarlet figure of the young Poins, working his hand into the boy's arm and whispering to him. The servers and disservers went to their work of clearing the board.

But Culpepper sat there without word or motion, so that none of those lords had any sport out of him. Some of them went away to roast pippins at the Widow Amnot's, some to speak with the alchemist that, on the roof, watched the stars. So one and the other left the room; the torches burned out, most of them, and, save for two lords of the Archbishop's following, who said boldly that they would watch and care for this man, because he was the Queen's cousin, and there might be advancement in it, Culpepper was left alone.

His sword he had not with him, but he had his dagger, and, just as he drew it, appearing about to stab himself in the heart, there ran across the hall the black figure of Lascelles, so that he appeared to have been watching through a window, and the two lords threw themselves upon Culpepper's arm. And all three began to tell him that there was better work for him to do than that of stabbing himself; and Lascelles brought with him a flagon of *aqua vitæ* from Holland, and poured out a little for Culpepper to drink. And one of the lords said that his room was up in the gallery near the Queen's, and, if Culpepper would go with him there, they might make good cheer. Only he must be silent in the going thither; afterwards it would not so much matter, for they would be past the guards. So, linking their arms in his, they wound up and across the courtyard, where the torchmen that waited on their company of diners to light them, blessed God that the sitting was over, and beat their torches out against the ground.

In the shadow of the high walls, and some in the moonlight, the serving-men held their parliament. They discoursed of these things, and some said that it was a great pity that T. Culpepper was come to Court. For he was an idle braggart, and where he was disorder grew, and that was a pity, since the Queen had made the Court orderly, and servants were little beaten. But some said that like sire was like child, and that great disorders there were in the Court, but quiet ones, and the Queen the centre. But these were mostly the cleaners of dishes and the women that swept rooms and spread new rushes. Upon the whole, the cooks blessed the Queen, along with all them that had to do with feeding and the kitchens. They thanked God for her because she had brought back the old fasts. For, as they argued, your fast brings honours to cooks, since, after a meagre day, your lord cometh to his trencher with a better appetite, and then is your cook commended. The Archbishop's cooks were the hottest in this contention, for they had the most reason to know. The stablemen, palfreniers, and falconers' mates were, most part of them, politicians more than the others, and these wondered to have seen, through their peep-holes and door-cracks, the Queen's cousin go away with these lords that were of the contrary party. Some said that T. Culpepper was her emissary to win them over to her interests, and some, that always cousins, uncles, and kin were the bitterest foes a Queen had, as witness the case of Queen Anne Boleyn and the Yellow Dog of Norfolk who had worked to ruin her. And some said it was marvellous that there they could sit or stand and talk of such things—for a year or so ago all the Court was spies, so that the haymen mistrusted them that forked down the straw, and meat-servers them with the wine. But now each man could talk as he would, and it made greatly for fellowship when a man could sit against a wall, unbutton in the warm nights, and say what he listed.

The light of the great fires grew dull in the line of kitchen windows; sweethearting couples came in through the great gateway from the grass-slopes beneath the castle walls. There was a little bustle when four horsemen rode in to say that the King's Highness was but nine miles from the castle, and torchmen must be there to light him in towards midnight. But the Queen should not be told for her greater pleasure and surprise. Then all these servingmen stood up and shook themselves, and said—"To bed." For, on the morrow, with the King back, there would surely be great doings and hard work. And to mews and kennels and huts, in the straw and beds of rushes, these men betook themselves. The young lords came back laughing from Widow Amnot's at the castle foot; there was not any light to be seen save one in all that courtyard full of windows. The King's torchmen slumbered in the guard-room where they awaited his approach. Darkness, silence, and deep shadow lay everywhere, though overhead the sky was pale with moonlight, and, from high in the air, the thin and silvery tones of the watchman's horn on the roof filtered down at the quarter hours. A drowsy bell marked the hours, and the cries and drillings of the night birds vibrated from very high.

V

Coming very late to her bedroom the Queen found awaiting her her tiring-maid, Mary Trelyon, whom she had advanced into the post that Margot Poins had held, and the old Lady Rochford.

"Why," she said to her maid, "when you have unlaced me you may go, or you will not love my service that keeps you so late."

Mary Trelyon cast her eyes on the ground, and said that it was such pleasure to attend her mistress, that not willingly would she give up that discoiffing, undoing of hair, and all the rest, for long she had desired to have the handling of these precious things and costly garments.

"No, you shall get you gone," the Queen said, "for I will not have you, sweetheart, be red-lidded in the morning with this long watching, for tomorrow the King comes, and I will have him see my women comely and fair, though in your love you will not care for yourselves."

Standing before her mirror, where there burned in silver dishes four tall candles with perfumed wicks, Katharine offered her back to the loosening fingers of this girl.

"I would not have you to think," she said, "that I am always thus late and a gadabout. But this day"—the Queen's eyes sparkled, and her cheeks were red with exaltation—"this day and this night are one that shall be marked with red stones in the calendar of England, and late have I travailed so to make them be."

The girl was very black-avised, and her face beneath her grey hood— for the Queen's maids were all in grey, with crowned roses, the device that the King had given her at their wedding, worked in red silk on each shoulder—her face beneath her grey hood was the clear shape of the thin end of an egg. She worked at the unlacing of the Queen's gown, so that she at last must kneel down to it.

Having finished, she remained upon her knees, but she twisted her fingers in her skirt as if she were bashful, yet her face was perturbed with red flushes on the dark cheeks.

The Queen, feeling that she knelt there upon her loosened gown and did not get her gone, said—

"Anan?"

"Please you let me stay," the girl said; but Katharine answered—

"I would commune with my own thoughts."

"Please you hear me," the girl said, and she was very earnest; but the Queen answered—

"Why, no! If you have any boon to ask of me, you know very well that tomorrow at eleven is the hour for asking. Now, I will sit still with the silence. Bring me my chair to the table. The Lady Rochford shall put out my lights when I be abed."

The girl stood up and rolled, with a trick of appeal, her eyes to the old Lady Rochford. This lady, all in grey too, but with a great white hood because she was a widow, sat back upon the foot of the great bed. Her face was perturbed, but it had been always perturbed since her cousin, the Queen Anne Boleyn, had fallen by the axe. She put a gouty and swollen finger to her lips, and the girl shrugged her shoulders with a passion of despair, for she was very hot-tempered, and it was as if mutinously that she fetched the Queen her chair and set it behind her where she stood before the mirror taking off her breast jewel from its chain. And again the girl shrugged her shoulders. Then she went to the little wall-door that corkscrewed down into the courtyard through the thick of the wall. Immediately after she was gone they heard the lockguard that awaited her without set on the great padlock without the door. Then his feet clanked down the stairway, he being heavily loaded with weighty keys. It was the doors along the corridor that the young Poins guarded, and these were never opened once the Queen was in her room, save by the King. The Lady Rochford slept in the anteroom upon a truckle-bed, and the great withdrawing-room was empty.

It was very still in the Queen's room and most shadowy, except before the mirror where the candle flames streamed upwards. The pillars of the great bed were twisted out of dark wood; the hangings of bed and walls were all of a dark blue arras, and the bedspread was of a dark red velvet worked in gold with pomegranates and pomegranate leaves. Only the pillows and the turnover of the sheets were of white linen-lawn, and the bed curtains nearly hid them with shadows. Where the Queen sat there was light like that of an altar in a dim chapel, for the room was so huge.

She sat before her glass, silently taking off her golden things. She took the jewel off the chain round her neck and laid it in a casket of gold and ivory. She took the rings off her fingers and hung them on the lance of a little knight in silver. She took off her waist where it hung to a brooch of feridets, her pomander of enamel and gold; she opened it and marked the time by the watch studded with sable diamonds that it held.

"Past eleven," she said, "if my watch goes right."

"Indeed it is past eleven," the Lady Rochford sighed behind her.

The Queen sat forward in her chair, looking deep into the shadows of her mirror. A great relaxation was in all her limbs, for she was very tired, so that though she was minded to let down her hair she did not begin to undo her coif, and though she desired to think, she had no thoughts. From far away there came a muffled sound as if a door had been roughly closed, and the Lady Rochford shot out a little sound between a scream and a sigh.

"Why, you are very affrighted," the Queen said. "One would think you feared robbers; but my guards are too good."

She began to unloosen from her hood her jewel, which was a rose fashioned out of pink shell work set with huge dewdrops of diamonds and crowned with a little crown of gold.

"God knows," she said, "I ha' trinkets enow for robbers. It takes me too long to undo them. I would the King did not so load me."

"Your Highness is too humble for a Queen," the old Lady Rochford grumbled. "Let me aid you, since the maid is gone. I would not have you speak your maids so humbly. My Cousin Anne that was the Queen—"

She came stiffly and heavily forward from the bed with her hands out to discoif her lady; but the Queen turned her head, caught at her fat hand, put it against her cheek and fondled it.

"I would have your Highness feared by all," the old lady said.

"I would have myself by all beloved," Katharine answered. "What, am I to play the Queen and Highness to such serving-maids as I was once the fellow and companion to?"

"Your Highness should not have sent the wench away," the old woman said.

"Well, you have taken on a very sour voice," the Queen said. "I will study to pleasure you more. Get you now back and rest you, for I know you stand uneasily, and you shall not uncoif me."

She began to unpin her coif, laying the golden pins in the silver candle-dishes. When her hair was thus set free of a covering, though it was smoothly braided and parted over her forehead, yet it was lightly rebellious, so that little mists of it caught the light, golden and rejoiceful. Her face was serious, her nose a little peaked, her lips rested lightly together, and her blue eyes steadily challenged their counterparts in the mirror with an assured and gentle glance.

"Why," she said, "I believe you have the right of it—but for a queen

I must be the same make of queen that I am as a woman. A queen gracious rather than a queen regnant; a queen to grant petitions rather than one to brush aside the petitioners."

She stopped and mused.

"Yet," she said, "you will do me the justice to say that in the open and in the light of day, when men are by or the King's presence demands it, I do ape as well as I may the painted queens of galleries and the stately ladies that are to be seen in pictured books."

"I would not have had you send away the maid," the old Lady Rochford said.

"God help me," the Queen answered. "I stayed her petition till the morrow. Is that not queening it enough?"

The Lady Rochford suddenly wrung her hands.

"I had rather," she said, "you had heard her and let her stay. Here there are not people enough to guard you. You should have many scores of people. This is a dreary place."

"Heaven help me," the Queen said. "If I were such a queen as to be affrighted, you would affright me. Tell me of your cousin that was a sinful queen."

The Lady Rochford raised her hands lamentably and bleated out—

"Ah God, not tonight!"

"You have been ready enough on other nights," the Queen said. And, indeed, it was so much the practice of this lady to talk always of her cousin, whose death had affrighted her, that often the Queen had begged her to cease. But tonight she was willing to hear, for she felt afraid of no omens, and, being joyful, was full of pity for the dead unfortunate. She began with slow, long motions to withdraw the great pins from her hair. The deep silence settled down again, and she hummed the melancholy and stately tune that goes with the words—

> *"When all the little hills are hid in snow,*
> *And all the small brown birds by frost are slain,*
> *And sad and slow*
> *The silly sheep do go,*
> *All seeking shelter to and fro—*
> *Come once again*
> *To these familiar, silent, misty lands—"*

And—

"Aye," she said; "to these ancient and familiar lands of the dear saints, please God, when the winter snows are upon them, once again shall come the feet of God's messenger, for this is the joyfullest day this land hath known since my namesake was cast down and died."

Suddenly there were muffled cries from beyond the thick door in the corridor, and on the door itself resounding blows. The Lady Rochford gave out great shrieks, more than her feeble body could have been deemed to hold.

"Body of God!" the Queen said, "what is this?"

"Your cousin!" the Lady Rochford cried out. She came running to the Queen, who, in standing up, had overset her heavy chair, and, falling to her knees, she babbled out—"Your cousin! Oh, let it not all come again. Call your guard. Let it not all come again"; and she clawed into the Queen's skirt, uttering incomprehensible clamours.

"What? What? What?" Katharine said.

"He was with the Archbishop. Your cousin with the Archbishop. I heard it. I sent to stay him if it were so"; and the old woman's teeth crackled within her jaws. "O God, it is come again!" she cried.

The door flung open heavily, but slowly, because it was so heavy. And, in the archway, whilst a great scream from the old woman wailed out down the corridors, Katharine was aware of a man in scarlet, locked in a struggle with a raging swirl of green manhood. The man in scarlet fell back, and then, crying out, ran away. The man in green, his bonnet off, his red hair sticking all up, his face pallid, and his eyes staring like those of a sleep-walker, entered the room. In his right hand he had a dagger. He walked very slowly.

The Queen thought fast: the old Lady Rochford had her mouth open; her eyes were upon the dagger in Culpepper's hand.

"I seek the Queen," he said, but his eyes were lacklustre; they fell upon Katharine's face as if they had no recognition, or could not see. She turned her body round to the old Lady Rochford, bending from the hips so as not to move her feet. She set her fingers upon her lips.

"I seek—I seek—" he said, and always he came closer to her. His eyes were upon her face, and the lids moved.

"I seek the Queen," he said, and beneath his husky voice there were bass notes of quivering anger, as if, just as he had been by chance calmed by throwing down the guard, so by chance his anger might arise again.

The Queen never moved, but stood up full and fair; one strand of her hair, loosened, fell low over her left ear. When he was so close to her that his protruded hips touched her skirt, she stole her hand slowly round him till it closed upon his wrist above the dagger. His mouth opened, his eyes distended.

"I seek—" he said, and then—"Kat!" as if the touch of her cool and firm fingers rather than the sight of her had told to his bruised senses who she was.

"Get you gone!" she said. "Give me your dagger." She uttered each word roundly and fully as if she were pondering the next move over a chequer-board.

"Well, I will kill the Queen," he said. "How may I do it without my knife?"

"Get you gone!" she said again. "I will direct you to the Queen."

He passed the back of his left hand wearily over his brow.

"Well, I have found thee, Kat!" he said.

She answered: "Aye!" and her fingers twined round his on the hilt of the dagger, so that his were loosening.

Then the old Lady Rochford screamed out—

"Ha! God's mercy! Guards, swords, come!" The furious blood came into Culpepper's face at the sound. His hand he tore from Katharine's, and with the dagger raised on high he ran back from her and then forward towards the Lady Rochford. With an old trick of fence, that she had learned when she was a child, Katharine Howard set out her foot before him, and, with the speed of his momentum, he pitched over forward. He fell upon his face so that his forehead was upon the Lady Rochford's right foot. His dagger he still grasped, but he lay prone with the drink and the fever.

"Now, by God in His mercy," Katharine said to her, "as I am the Queen I charge you—"

"Take his knife and stab him to the heart!" the Lady Rochford cried out. "This will slay us two."

"I charge you that you listen to me," the Queen said, "or, by God, I will have you in chains!"

"I will call your many," the Lady Rochford cried out, for terror had stopped up the way from her ears to her brain, and she made towards the door. But Katharine set her hand to the old woman's shoulder.

"Call no man," she commanded. "This is a device of mine enemies to have men see this of me."

"I will not stay here to be slain," the old woman said.

"Then mine own self will slay you," the Queen answered. Culpepper moved in his stupor. "Before Heaven," the Queen said, "stay you there, and he shall not again stand up."

"I will go call—" the old woman besought her, and again Culpepper moved. The Queen stood right up against her; her breast heaved, her face was rigid. Suddenly she turned and ran to the door. That key she wrenched round and out, and then to the other door beside it, and that key too she wrenched round and out.

"I will not stay alone with my cousin," she said, "for that is what mine enemies would have. And this I vow, that if again you squeak I will have you tried as being an abettor of this treason." She went and knelt down at her cousin's head; she moved his face round till it was upon her lap.

"Poor Tom," she said; he opened his eyes and muttered stupid words.

She looked again at Lady Rochford.

"All this is nothing," she said, "if you will hide in the shadow of the bed and keep still. I have seen my cousin a hundred times thus muddied with drink, and do not fear him. He shall not stand up till he is ready to go through the door; but I will not be alone with him and tend him."

The Lady Rochford waddled and quaked like a jelly to the shadow of the bed curtains. She pulled back the curtain over the window, and, as if the contact with the world without would help her, threw back the casement. Below, in the black night, a row of torches shook and trembled, like little planets, in the distance.

Katharine Howard held her cousin's head upon her knees. She had seen him thus a hundred times and had no fear of him. For thus in his cups, and fevered as he was with ague that he had had since a child, he was always amenable to her voice though all else in the world enraged him. So that, if she could keep the Lady Rochford still, she might well win him out through the door at which he came in.

And, first, when he moved to come to his knees, she whispered—

"Lie down, lie down," and he set one elbow on to the carpet and lay over on his side, then on his back. She took his head again on to her lap, and with soft motions reached to take the dagger from his hand. He yielded it up and gazed upwards into her face.

"Kat!" he said, and she answered—

"Aye!"

There came from very far the sound of a horn.

"When you can stand," she said, "you must get you gone."

"I have sold farms to get you gowns," he answered.

"And then we came to Court," she said, "to grow great."

He passed his left hand once more over his eyes with a gesture of ineffable weariness, but his other arm that was extended, she knelt upon.

"Now we are great," she said.

He muttered, "I wooed thee in an apple orchard. Let us go back to Lincolnshire."

"Why, we will talk of it in the morning," she said. "It is very late."

Her brain throbbed with the pulsing blood. She was set to get him gone before the young Poins could call men to her door. It was maddeningly strange to think that none hitherto had come. Maybe Culpepper had struck him dead with his knife, or he lay without fainting. This black enigma, calling for haste that she dare not show, filled all the shadows of that shadowy room.

"It is very late," she said, "you must get you gone. It was compacted between us that ever you would get you gone early."

"Aye, I would not have thee shamed," he said. He spoke upwards, slowly and luxuriously, his head so softly pillowed, his eyes gazing at the ceiling. He had never been so easy in two years past. "I remember that was the occasion of our pact. I did wooe thee in an apple orchard to the grunting of hogs."

"Get you gone," she said; "buy me a favour against the morning."

"Why," he said, "I am a very rich lord. I have lands in Kent now. I will buy thee such a gown. . . such a gown. . . The hogs grunted. . . There is a song about it. . . Let me go to buy thy gown. Aye, now, presently. I remember a great many things. As thus. . . there is a song of a lady loved a swine. Honey, said she, and hunc, said he."

Whilst she listened a great many thoughts came into her mind—of their youth at home, where indeed, to the grunting of hogs, he had wooed her when she came out from conning her Plautus with the Magister. And at the same time it troubled her to consider where the young Poins had bestowed himself. Maybe he was dead; maybe he lay in a faint.

"It was in our pact," she said to Culpepper, "that you should get you gone ever when I would have it."

"Aye, sure, it was in our pact," he said.

He closed his eyes as if he would fall asleep, being very weary and come to his desired haven. Above his closed eyes Katharine threw the key of her antechamber on to the bed. She pointed with her hand to that door that the Lady Rochford should undo. If she could get her cousin through that door—and now he was in the mood—if she could but get him through there and out at the door beyond the Big Room into the corridor, before her guard came back. . .

But the Lady Rochford was leaning far out beyond the window-sill and did not see her gesture.

Culpepper muttered—

"Ah; well; aye; even so—" And from the window came a scream that tore the air—

"The King! the King!"

And immediately it was as if the life of a demon had possessed Culpepper in all his limbs.

"Merciful God!" the Queen cried out. "I am patient."

Culpepper had writhed from her till he sat up, but she hollowed her hand around his throat. His head she forced back till she held it upon the floor, and whilst he writhed with his legs she knelt upon his chest with one knee. He screamed out words like: "Bawd," and "Ilcock," and "Hecate," and the Lady Rochford screamed—

"The King comes! the King comes!"

Then Katharine said within herself—

"Is it this to be a Queen?"

She set both her hands upon his neck and pressed down the whole weight of her frame, till the voice died in his throat. His body stirred beneath her knee, convulsively, so that it was as if she rode a horse. His eyes, as slowly he strangled, glared hideously at the ceiling, from which the carven face of a Queen looked down into them. At last he lay still, and Katharine Howard rose up.

She ran at the old woman—

"God forgive me if I have killed my cousin," she said. "I am certain that now He will forgive me if I slay thee." And she had Culpepper's dagger in her hand.

"For," she said, "I stand for Christ His cause: I will not be undone by meddlers. Hold thy peace!"

The Lady Rochford opened her mouth to speak.

"Hold thy peace!" the Queen said again, and she lifted up the dagger. "Speak not. Do as I bid thee. Answer me when I ask. For this I swear as I am the Queen that, since I have the power to slay whom I will and none question it, I will slay thee if thou do not my bidding."

The old woman trembled lamentably.

"Where is the King come to?" the Queen said.

"Even to the great gate; he is out of sight," was her answer.

"Come now," the Queen commanded. "Let us drag my cousin behind my table."

"Shall he be hidden there?" the Lady Rochford cried out. "Let us cast him from the window."

"Hold your peace," the Queen cried out. "Speak you never one word more. But come!"

She took her cousin by the arm, the Lady Rochford took him by the other and they dragged him, inert and senseless, into the shadow of the Queen's mirror table.

"Pray God the King comes soon," the Queen said. She stood above her cousin and looked down upon him. A great pitifulness came into her face.

"Loosen his shirt," she said. "Feel if his heart beats!"

The Lady Rochford had a face full of fear and repulsion.

"Loosen his shirt. Feel if his heart beats," the Queen said. "And oh!" she added, "woe shall fall upon thee if he be dead."

She reflected a moment to think upon how long it should be ere the King came to her door. Then she raised her chair, and sat down at her mirror. For one minute she set her face into her hands; then she began to straighten herself, and with her hands behind her to tighten the laces of her dress.

"For," she continued to Lady Rochford, "I do hold thee more guilty of his death than himself. He is but a drunkard in his cups, thou a palterer in sobriety."

She set her cap upon her head and smoothed the hair beneath it. In all her movements there was a great swiftness and decision. She set the jewel in her cap, the pomander at her side, the chain around her neck, the jewel at her breast.

"His heart beats," the Lady Rochford said, from her knees at Culpepper's side.

"Then thank the saints," Katharine answered, "and do up again his shirt."

She hurried in her attiring, and uttered engrossed commands.

"Kneel thou there by his side. If he stir or mutter before the King be in and the door closed, put thy hand across his mouth."

"But the King—" the Lady Rochford said. "And—"

"Merciful God!" Katharine cried out again. "I am the Queen. Kneel there."

The Lady Rochford trembled down upon her knees; she was in fear for her life by the axe if the King came in.

"I thank God that the King is come," the Queen said. "If he had not, this man must have gone from hence in the sight of other men. So I will pardon thee for having cried out if now thou hold him silent till the King be in."

There came from very near a blare of trumpets. Katharine rose up, and went again to gaze upon her cousin. The dagger she laid upon her table.

"He may hold still yet," she said. "But I charge you that you muzzle him if he move or squeak."

There came great blows upon the door, and through the heavy wood, the Ha-ha of many voices. Slowly the Queen moved to the bed, and from it took the key where she had thrown it. There came again the heavy knocking, and she unlocked the door, slowly still.

In the corridor there were many torches, and beneath them the figure of the King in scarlet. Behind him was Norfolk all in black and with his yellow face, and Cranmer in black and with his anxious eyes, and behind them many other lords. The King came in, and, slow and stately, the Queen went down on her knees to greet him. The torch-light shone upon her jewels and her garments; her fair face was immobile, and her eyes upon the ground. The King raised her up, bent his knee to her, and kissed her on the hands, and so, turning to the men without, he uttered, roundly and fully, and his cheeks were ruddy with joy, and his eyes smiled—

"My lords, I am beholden to the King o' Scots. For had he met me I had not yet been here. Get you to your beds; I could wish ye had such wives—"

"The King! the King!" a voice muttered.

Henry said—

"Ha, who spoke?"

There was a faint squeak, a dull rustle.

"My cousin Kat—" the voice said.

The King said—

"Ha!" again, and incredulous and haughty he raised his brows.

Above the mirror, in the great light of the candles, there showed the pale face, the fishy, wide-open and bewildered eyes of Culpepper. His hair was dishevelled in points; his mouth was open in amazement. He uttered—

"The King!" as if that were the most astonishing thing, and, standing behind the table, staggered and clutched the arras to sustain himself.

Henry said—

"Ha! Treason!"

But Katharine whispered at his ear—

"No; this my cousin is distraught. Speak on to the lords."

In the King's long pause several lords said aloud—

"The King cried 'Treason!' Draw your swords!"

Then the King cast his cap upon the ground.

"By God!" he said. "What marlocking is this? Is it general joy that emboldens ye to this license? God help me!" he said, and he stamped his foot upon the ground—"Body of God!" And many other oaths he uttered. Then, with a sudden clutching at his throat, he called out—

"Well! well! I pardon ye. For no doubt to some that be young—and to some that be old too—it is an occasion for mummeries and japes when a good man cometh home to his dame."

He looked round upon Culpepper. The Queen's cousin stood, his jaw still hanging wide, and his body crumpled back against the arras. He was hidden from them all by wall and door, but Henry could not judge how long he would there remain. Riding through the night he had conned a speech that he would have said at the Queen's door, and at the times of joy and graciousness he loved to deliver great speeches. But there he said only—

"Why, God keep you. I thank such of you as were with me upon the campaign and journey. Now this campaign and journey is ended—I dissolve you each to his housing and bed. Farewell. Be as content as I be!"

And, with his great hand he swung to the heavy door.

PART III
THE DWINDLING MELODY

I

The Lady Rochford lay back upon the floor in a great faint.

"Heaven help me!" the Queen said. "I had rather she had played the villain than been such a palterer." She glided to the table and picked up the dagger that shone there beneath Culpepper's nose. "Take even this," she said to the King. "It is an ill thing to bestow. Sword he hath none."

Having had such an estimation of his good wife's wit that, since he would not have her think him a dullard, he passed over the first question that he would have asked, such as, "I think this be thy cousin and how came he here?"

"Would he have slain me?" he asked instead, as if it were a little thing.

"I do not think so," Katharine said. "Maybe it was me he would have slain."

"Body of God!" the King said sardonically. "He cometh for no cheap goods."

He had so often questioned his wife of this cousin of hers that he had his measure indifferent well.

"Why," the Queen said, "I do not know that he would have slain me. Maybe it was to save me from dragons that he came with his knife. He was, I think, with the Archbishop's men and came here very drunk. I would pray your Highness' Grace to punish him not over much for he is my mother's nephew and the only friend I had when I was very poor and a young child."

The King hung his head on his chest, and his rustic eyes surveyed the ground.

"I would have you to think," she said, "that he has been among evil men that advised and prompted him thus to assault my door. They would ruin and undo him and me."

"Well I know it," Henry said. He rubbed his hand up his left side, opened it and dropped it again—a trick he had when he thought deeply.

"The Archbishop," he said, "babbled somewhat—I know not what—of a cousin of thine that was come from the Scots, he thought, without leave or license."

"But how to get him hence, that my foes triumph not?" the Queen said, "for I would not have them triumph."

"I do think upon it," the King said.

"You are better at it than I," she answered.

Culpepper stood there at gaze, as if he were a corpse about which they talked. But the speaking of the Queen to another man excited him to gurgle and snarl in his throat like an ape. Then another mood coming into the channels of his brain—

"It was the King my cousin Kate did marry. This then is the Queen; I had pacted with myself to forget this Queen." He spoke straight out before him with the echo of thoughts that he had had during his exile.

"Ho!" the King said and smote his thigh. "It is plain what to do," and in spite of his scarlet and his bulk he had the air of a heavy but very cunning peasant. He reflected for a little more.

"It fits very well," he brought out. "This man must be richly rewarded."

"Why," Katharine said; "I had nigh strangled him. It makes me tremble to think how nigh I had strangled him. I would well he were rewarded."

The King considered his wife's cousin.

"Sirrah," he said, "we believe that thou canst not kneel, or kneeling, couldst not well again arise."

Culpepper regarded him with wide, blue, and uncomprehending eyes.

"So, thou standing as thou makest shift to do, we do make thee the keeper of this our Queen's ante-room."

He spoke with a pleasant and ironical glee, since it joyed him thus to gibe at one that had loved his wife. He—with his own prowess—had carried her off.

"Master Culpepper," he said—"or Sir Thomas—for I remember to have knighted you—if you can walk, now walk."

Culpepper muttered—

"The King! Why the King did wed my cousin Kat!"

And again—

"I must be circumspect. Oh aye, I must be circumspect or all is lost." For that was one of the things which in Scotland he had again and again impressed upon himself. "But in Lincoln, in bygone times, of a summer's night—"

"Poor Tom!" the Queen said; "once this fellow did wooe me."

Great tears gathered in Culpepper's eyes. They overflowed and rolled down his cheeks.

"In the apple-orchard," he said, "to the grunting of hogs. . . for the hogs were below the orchard wall. . ."

The King was pleased to think that it had been in his power to raise this lady an infinite distance above the wooing of this poor lout. It gave him an interlude of comedy. But though he set his hands on his hips and chuckled, he was a man too ready for action to leave much time for enjoyment.

"Why weep?" he said to Culpepper. "We have advanced thee to the Queen's ante-chamber. Come up thither."

He approached to Culpepper behind the mirror table and caught him by the arm. The poor drunkard, his face pallid, shrank away from this great bulk of shining scarlet. His eyes moved lamentably round the chamber and rested first upon Katharine, then upon the King.

"Which of us was it you would ha' killed?" the King said, to show the Queen how brave he was in thus handling a madman. And, being very strong, he dragged the swaying drunkard, who held back and whose head wagged on his shoulders, towards the door.

"Guard ho!" he called out, and before the door there stood three of his own men in scarlet and with pikes.

"Ho, where is the Queen's door-ward?" he called with a great voice. Before him, from the door side, there came the young Poins; his face was like chalk; he had a bruise above his eyes; his knees trembled beneath him.

"Ho thou!" the King said, "who art thou that would hinder my messenger from coming to the Queen?"

He stood back upon his feet; he clutched the drunkard in his great fist; his eyes started dreadfully.

The young Poins' lips moved, but no sound came out.

"This was my messenger," the King said, "and you hindered him. Body of God! Body of God!" and he made his voice to tremble as if with rage, whilst he told this lie to save his wife's fair fame. "Where have you been? Where have you tarried? What treason is this? For either you knew this was my messenger—as well I would have you know that he is—and it was treason and death to stay him. Or, if because he was drunk and speechless—as well he might be having travelled far and with expedition—ye did not know he was my messenger; then wherefore did ye not run to raise all the castle for succour?"

The young Poins pointed to the wound above his eye and then to the ground of the corridor. He would signify that Culpepper had struck him, and that there, on the ground, he had lain senseless.

"Ho!" the King said, for he was willing to know how many men in that castle had wind of this mischance. "You lay not there all this while. When I came here along, you stood here by the door in your place."

The young Poins fell upon his knees. He shook more violently than a naked man on a frosty day. For here indeed was the centre of his treason, since Lascelles had bidden him stay there, once Culpepper was in the Queen's room, and to say later that there the Queen had bidden him stay whilst she had her lover. And now, before the King's tremendous presence, he had the fear at his heart that the King knew this.

"Wherefore! wherefore!" the King thundered, "wherefore didst not cry out—cry out—'Treason, Raise the watch!'? Hail out aloud?"

He waited, silent for a long time. The three pikemen leaned upon their pikes; and now Culpepper had fallen against the door-post, where the King held him up. And behind his back the Queen marvelled at the King's ready wit. This was the best stroke that ever she had known him do. And the Lady Rochford lay where she had feigned to faint, straining her ears.

With all these ears listening for his words the young Poins knelt, his teeth chattering like burning wood that crackles.

"Wherefore? wherefore?" the King cried again.

Half inaudibly, his eyes upon the ground, the boy mumbled, "It was to save the Queen from scandal!"

The King let his jaw fall, in a fine aping of amazement. Then, with the huge swiftness of a bull, he threw Culpepper towards one of the guards, and, leaning over, had the kneeling boy by the throat.

"Scandal!" he said. "Body of God! Scandal!" And the boy screamed out, and raised his hands to hide the King's intolerable great face that blazed down over his eyes.

The huge man cast him from him, so that he fell over backwards, and lay upon his side.

"Scandal!" the King cried out to his guards. "Here is a pretty scandal! That a King may not send a messenger to his wife withouten scandal! God help me. . ."

He stood suddenly again over the boy as if he would trample him to a shapeless pulp. But, trembling there, he stepped back.

"Up, bastard!" he called out. "Run as ye never ran. Fetch hither the Lord d'Espahn and His Grace of Canterbury, that should have ordered these matters."

FORD MADOX FORD

The boy stumbled to his knees, and then, a flash of scarlet, ran, his head down, as if eagles were tearing at his hair.

The King turned upon his guard.

"Ho!" he said, "you, Jenkins, stay here with this my knight cousin. You, Cale and Richards, run to fetch a launderer that shall set a mattress in the ante-chamber for this my cousin to lie on. For this my cousin is the Queen's chamber-ward, and shall there lie when I am here, if so be I have occasion for a messenger at night."

The two guards ran off, striking upon the ground before them as they ran the heavy staves of their pikes. This noise was intended to warn all to make way for his Highness' errand-bearers.

"Why," the King said pleasantly to Jenkins, a guard with a blond and shaven face whom he liked well, "let us set this gentleman against the wall in the ante-room till his bed be come. He hath earned gentle usage, since he hasted much, bringing my message from Scotland to the Queen, and is very ill."

So, helping his guard gently to conduct the drunkard into his wife's dark ante-room, the King came out again to his wife.

"Is it well done?" he asked.

"Marvellous well done," she answered.

"I am the man for these difficult times!" he answered, and was glad.

The Queen sighed a little. For if she admired and wondered at her lord's power skilfully to have his way, it made her sad to think—as she must think—that so devious was man's work.

"I would," she said, "that it was not to such an occasion that I spurred thee."

Her eyes, being cast downwards, fell upon the Lady Rochford, by the table.

"Ho, get up," she cried. "You have feigned fainting long enough. But for you all this had been more easy. I would have you relieve mine eyes of the sight of your face." She moved to aid the old woman to rise, but before she was upon her knees there stood without the door both the Lord d'Espahn and the Archbishop. They had waited just beyond the corridor-end with a great many of the other lords, all afraid of mysteries they knew not what, and thus it was that they came so soon upon the young Poins' summoning.

II

The King thought fit to change his mood, so that it was with uplifted brows and a quizzing smile at the corners of his mouth that for a minute he greeted these frightened lords in the doorway. They stood there silent, the Archbishop very dejected, the Lord d'Espahn, with his grey beard, very erect and ruddy featured.

"Why, God help me," the King said, "what make of Court is this of mine where a King may not send a messenger to his wife?"

The Archbishop swallowed in his throat; the Lord d'Espahn did not speak but gazed before him.

"You shall tell me what befell, for I am ignorant," the King said; "but first I will tell you what I do know."

"Why, come out with me into the corridor, wife," he cried over his shoulder. "For it is not fitting that these lords come into thy apartment. I will walk with them and talk."

He took the Archbishop by the elbow and the Lord d'Espahn by the upper arm, and, leaning upon them, propelled them gently before him.

"Thus it was," he said; "this cousin of my wife's was in the King o' Scots' good town of Edinboro'. And, being there, he was much upon my conscience—for I would not have a cousin of my wife's be there in exile, he being one that formerly much fended for her. . ."

He spoke out his words and repeated these things for his own purposes, the Queen following behind. When they were come to the corridor-end, there he found, as he had thought, a knot of lords and gentlemen, babbling with their ears pricked up.

"Nay, stay," he said, "this is a matter that all may hear."

There were there the Duke of Norfolk and his son, young Surrey with the vacant mouth, Sir Henry Wriothesley with the great yellow beard, the Lord Dacre of the North, the old knight Sir N. Rochford, Sir Henry Peel of these parts, with a many of their servants, amongst them Lascelles. Most of them were in scarlet or purple, but many were in black. The Earl of Surrey had the Queen's favour of a crowned rose in his bonnet, for he was of her party. The gallery opened out there till it was as big as a large room, broad and low-ceiled, and lit with torches in irons at the angles of it. On rainy days the Queen's maids were here accustomed to play at stool-ball.

"This is a matter that all may hear," the King said, "and some shall render account." He let the Lord d'Espahn and the Archbishop go, so that they faced him. The Queen looked over his shoulder.

"As thus. . ." he said.

And he repeated how it had lain upon his conscience and near his heart that the Queen's good cousin languished in the town of Edinburgh.

"And how near we came to Edinboro' those of ye that were with me can make account."

And, lying there, he had taken occasion to send a messenger with others that went to the King o' Scots—to send a messenger with letters unto this T. Culpepper. One letter was to bid him hasten home unto the Queen, and one was a letter that he should bear.

"For," said the King, "we thought thus—as ye wist—that the King o' Scots would come obedient to our summoning and that there we should lie some days awaiting and entertaining him. Thus did I wish to send my Queen swift message of our faring, and I was willing that this, her cousin and mine, should be my postman and messenger. For he should—I bade him—set sail in a swift ship for these coasts and so come quicker than ever a man might by land."

He paused to observe the effect of his words, but no lord spoke though some whispered amongst themselves.

"Now," he said, "what stood within my letter to the Queen was this, after salutations, that she should reward this her cousin that in the aforetime had much fended for her when she was a child. For I was aware how, out of a great delicacy and fear of nepotism, such as was shown by certain of the Popes now dead, she raised up none of her relations and blood, nor none that before had aided her when she was a child and poor. But I was willing that this should be otherwise, and they be much helped that before had helped her since now she helpeth me and assuageth my many and fell labours."

He paused and went a step back that he might stand beside the Queen, and there, before them all, Katharine was most glad that she had again set on all her jewels and was queen-like. She had composed her features, and gazed before her over their heads, her hands being folded in the lap of her gown.

"Now," the King said, "this letter of mine was a little thing—but great maybe, since it bore my will. Yet"—and he made his voice minatory—"in these evil and tickle times well it might have been that that letter held delicate news. Then all my plots had gone to ruin. How came it that some of ye—I know not whom!—thus letted and hindered my messenger?"

He had raised his voice very high. He stayed it suddenly, and some there shivered.

He uttered balefully, "Anan!"

"As Christ is my Saviour," the Lord d'Espahn said, "I, since I am the Queen's Marshal, am answerable in this, as well I know. Yet never saw I this man till tonight at supper. He would have my seat then, and I gave it him. Ne let ne hindrance had he of me, but went his way where and when he would."

"You did very well," the King said. "Who else speaks?"

The Archbishop looked over his shoulder, and with a dry mouth uttered, "Lascelles!"

Lascelles, deft and blond and gay, shouldered his way through that unwilling crowd, and fell upon his knees.

"Of this I know something," he said; "and if any have offended, doubtless it is I, though with good will."

"Well, speak!" the King said.

Lascelles recounted how the Queen, riding out, had seen afar this gentleman lying amid the heather.

"And if she should not know him who was her cousin, how should we who are servants?" he said. But, having heard that the Queen would have this poor, robbed wayfarer tended and comforted, he, Lascelles, out of the love and loyalty he owed her Grace, had so tended and so comforted him that he had given up to him his own bed and board. But it was not till that day that, Culpepper being washed and apparelled—not till that day a little before supper, had he known him for Culpepper, the Queen's cousin. So he had gone with him that night to the banquet-hall, and there had served him, and, after, had attended him with some lords and gentles. But, at the last, Culpepper had shaken them off and bidden them leave him.

"And who were we, what warrants had we, to restrain the Queen's noble cousin?" he finished. "And, as for letters, I never saw one, though all his apparel, in rags, was in my hands. I think he must have lost this letter amongst the robbers he fell in with. But what I could do, I did for love of the Queen's Grace, who much hath favoured me."

The King studied his words. He looked at the Queen's face and then at those of the lords before him.

"Why, this tale hath a better shewing," he said. "Herein appeareth that none, save the Queen's door-ward, came ever against this good knight and cousin of mine. And, since this knight was in liquor, and not overwise sensible—as well he might be after supping in moors and deserts—maybe that door-ward had his reasonable reasonings."

He paused again, and looking upon the Queen's face for a sign:

"If it be thus, it is well," he said, "I will pardon and assoil you all, if later it shall appear that this is the true truth."

Lascelles whispered in the Archbishop's ear, and Cranmer uttered—

"The witnesses be here to prove it, if your Highness will."

"Why," the King said, "it is late enough," and he leered at Cranmer, for whom he had an affection. He looked again upon the Queen to see how fair she was and how bravely she bore herself, upright and without emotion. "This wife of mine," he said, "is ever of the pardoning side. If ye had so injured me I had been among ye with fines and amercements. But she, I perceive, will not have it so, and I am too glad to be smiled upon now to cross her will. So, get you gone and sleep well. But, before you go, I will have you listen to some words. . ."

He cleared his throat, and in his left hand took the Queen's.

"Know ye," he said, "that I am as proud of this my Queen as was ever mother of her first-born child. For lo, even as the Latin poet saith, that, upon bearing a child, many evil women are led to repentance and right paths, so have I, your King, been led towards righteousness by wedding of this lady. For I tell you that, but for certain small hindrances—and mostly this treacherous disloyalty of the King o' Scots that thus with his craven marrow hath featorously dallied to look upon my face—but for that and other small things there had gone forth this night through the dark to the Bishop of Rome certain tidings that, please God, had made you and me and all this land the gladdest that be in Christendom. And this I tell you, too, that though by this misadventure and fear of the King o' Scots, these tidings have been delayed, yet is it only for a little space and, full surely, that day cometh. And for this you shall give thanks first to God and then to this royal lady here. For she, before all things, having the love of God in her heart, hath brought about this desired consummation. And this I say, to her greater praise, here in the midmost of you all, that it be noised unto the utmost corners of the world how good a Queen the King hath taken to wife."

The Queen had stood very motionless in the bright illuminations and dancings of the torches. But at the news of delay, through the King of Scots, a spasm of pain and concern came into her face. So that, if her features did not again move they had in them a savour of anguish, her eyebrows drooping, and the corners of her mouth.

"And now, good-night!" the King pursued with raised tones. "If ever ye slept well since these troublous times began, now ye may sleep well in the drowsy night. For now, in this my reign, are come the shortening years like autumn days. Now I will have such peace in land as cometh to the husbandman. He hath ingarnered his grain; he hath barned his fodder and straw; his sheep are in the byres and in the stalls his oxen. So, sitteth he by his fireside with wife and child, and hath no fear of winter. Such a man am I, your King, who in the years to come shall rest in peace."

The lords and gentlemen made their reverences, bows and knees; they swept round in their coloured assembly, and the Queen stood very tall and straight, watching their departure with saddened eyes.

The King was very gay and caught her by the waist.

"God help me, it is very late," he said. "Hearken!"

From above the corridor there came the drowsy sound of the clock.

"Thy daughter hath made her submission," the Queen said. "I had thought this was the gladdest day in my life."

"Why, so it is," he said, "as now day passeth to day." The clock ceased. "Every day shall be glad," he said, "and gladder than the rest."

At her chamber door he made a bustle. He would have the Queen's women come to untire her, a leech to see to Culpepper's recovery. He was willing to drink mulled wine before he slept. He was afraid to talk with his wife of delaying his letter to Rome. That was why he had told the news before her to his lords.

He fell upon the Lady Rochford that stood, not daring to go, within the Queen's room. He bade her sit all night by the bedside of T. Culpepper; he reviled her for a craven coward that had discountenanced the Queen. She should pay for it by watching all night, and woe betide her if any had speech with T. Culpepper before the King rose.

III

D own in the lower castle, the Archbishop was accustomed, when he undressed, to have with him neither priest nor page, but only, when he desired to converse of public matters—as now he did—his gentleman, Lascelles. He knelt above his kneeling-stool of black wood; he was telling his beads before a great crucifix with an ivory Son of God upon it. His chamber had bare white walls, his bed no curtains, and all the other furnishing of the room was a great black lectern whereto there was chained a huge Book of the Holy Writ that had his Preface. The tears were in his eyes as he muttered his prayers; he glanced upwards at the face of his Saviour, who looked down with a pallid, uncoloured face of ivory, the features shewing a great agony so that the mouth was opened. It was said that this image, that came from Italy, had had a face serene, before the Queen Katharine of Aragon had been put away. Then it had cried out once, and so remained ever lachrymose and in agony.

"God help me, I cannot well pray," the Archbishop said. "The peril that we have been in stays with me still."

"Why, thank God that we are come out of it very well," Lascelles said. "You may pray and then sleep more calm than ever you have done this sennight."

He leant back against the reading-pulpit, and had his arm across the Bible as if it had been the shoulder of a friend.

"Why," the Archbishop said, "this is the worst day ever I have been through since Cromwell fell."

"Please it your Grace," his confidant said, "it shall yet turn out the best."

The Archbishop faced round upon his knees; he had taken off the jewel from before his breast, and, with his chain of Chaplain of the George, it dangled across the corner of the fald-stool. His coat was unbuttoned at the neck, his robe open, and it was manifest that his sleeves of lawn were but sleeves, for in the opening was visible, harsh and grey, the shirt of hair that night and day he wore.

"I am weary of this talk of the world," he said. "Pray you begone and leave me to my prayers."

"Please it your Grace to let me stay and hearten you," Lascelles said, and he was aware that the Archbishop was afraid to be alone with the white Christ. "All your other gentry are in bed. I shall watch your sleep, to wake you if you cry out."

And in his fear of Cromwell's ghost that came to him in his dreams, the Archbishop sighed—

"Why stay, but speak not. Y'are over bold."

He turned again to the wall; his beads clicked; he sighed and remained still for a long time, a black shadow, huddled together in a black gown, sighing before the white and lamenting image that hung above him.

"God help me," he said at last. "Tell me why you say this is *dies felix*?"

Lascelles, who smiled for ever and without mirth, said—

"For two things: firstly, because this letter and its sending are put off. And secondly, because the Queen is—patently and to all people—proved lewd."

The Archbishop swung his head round upon his shoulders.

"You dare not say it!" he said.

"Why, the late Queen Katharine from Aragon was accounted a model of piety, yet all men know she was over fond with her confessor," Lascelles smiled.

"It is an approved lie and slander," the Archbishop said.

"It served mightily well in pulling down that Katharine," his confidant answered.

"One day"—the Archbishop shivered within his robes—"the account and retribution for these lies shall be to be paid. For well we know, you, I, and all of us, that these be falsities and cozenings."

"Marry," Lascelles said, "of this Queen it is now sufficiently proved true."

The Archbishop made as if he washed his hands.

"Why," Lascelles said, "what man shall believe it was by chance and accident that she met her cousin on these moors? She is not a compass that pointeth, of miraculous power, true North."

"No good man shall believe what you do say," the Archbishop cried out.

"But a multitude of indifferent will," Lascelles answered.

"God help me," the Archbishop said, "what a devil you are that thus hold out and hold out for ever hopes."

"Why," Lascelles said, "I think you were well helped that day that I came into your service. It was the Great Privy Seal that bade me serve you and commended me."

The Archbishop shivered at that name.

"What an end had Thomas Cromwell!" he said.

"Why, such an end shall not be yours whilst this King lives, so well he loves you," Lascelles answered.

The Archbishop stood upon his feet; he raised his hands above his head.

"Begone! Begone!" he cried. "I will not be of your evil schemes."

"Your Grace shall not," Lascelles said very softly, "if they miscarry. But when it is proven to the hilt that this Queen is a very lewd woman—and proven it shall be—your Grace may carry an accusation to the King—"

Cranmer said—

"Never! never! Shall I come between the lion and his food?"

"It were better if your Grace would carry the accusation," Lascelles uttered nonchalantly, "for the King will better hearken to you than to any other. But another man will do it too."

"I will not be of this plotting," the Archbishop cried out. "It is a very wicked thing!" He looked round at the white Christ that, upon the dark cross, bent anguished brows upon him. "Give me strength," he said.

"Why, your Grace shall not be of it," Lascelles answered, "until it is proven in the eyes of your Grace—ay, and in the eyes of some of the Papist Lords—as, for instance, her very uncle—that this Queen was evil in her life before the King took her, and that she hath acted very suspicious in the aftertime."

"You shall not prove it to the Papist Lords," Cranmer said. "It is a folly."

He added vehemently—

"It is a wicked plot. It is a folly too. I will not be of it."

"This is a very fortunate day," Lascelles said. "I think it is proven to all discerning men that that letter to him of Rome shall never be sent."

"Why, it is as plain as the truths of the Six Articles," Cranmer remonstrated, "that it shall be sent tomorrow or the next day. Get you gone! This King hath but the will of the Queen to guide him, and all her will turns upon that letter. Get you gone!"

"Please it your Grace," the spy said, "it is very manifest that with the Queen so it is. But with the King it is otherwise. He will pleasure the Queen if he may. But—mark me well—for this is a subtle matter—"

"I will not mark you," the Archbishop said. "Get you gone and find another master. I will not hear you. This is the very end."

Lascelles moved his arm from the Bible. He bent his form to a bow—he moved till his hand was on the latch of the door.

"Why, continue," the Archbishop said. "If you have awakened my fears, you shall slake them if you can—for this night I shall not sleep."

And so, very lengthily, Lascelles unfolded his view of the King's nature. For, said he, if this alliance with the Pope should come, it must be an alliance with the Pope and the Emperor Charles. For the King of France was an atheist, as all men knew. And an alliance with the Pope and the Emperor must be an alliance against France. But the King o' Scots was the closest ally that Francis had, and never should the King dare to wage war upon Francis till the King o' Scots was placated or wooed by treachery to be a prisoner, as the King would have made him if James had come into England to the meeting. Well would the King, to save his soul, placate and cosset his wife. But that he never dare do whilst James was potent at his back.

And again, Lascelles said, well knew the Archbishop that the Duke of Norfolk and his following were the ancient friends of France. If the Queen should force the King to this Imperial League, it must turn Norfolk and the Bishop of Winchester for ever to her bitter foes in that land. And along with them all the Protestant nobles and all the Papists too that had lands of the Church.

The Archbishop had been marking his words very eagerly. But suddenly he cried out—

"But the King! The King! What shall it boot if all these be against her so the King be but for her?"

"Why," Lascelles said, "this King is not a very stable man. Still, man he is, a man very jealous and afraid of fleers and flouts. If we can show him—I do accede to it that after what he hath done tonight it shall not be easy, but we may accomplish it—if before this letter is sent we may show him that all his land cries out at him and mocks him with a great laughter because of his wife's evil ways—why then, though in his heart he may believe her as innocent as you or I do now, it shall not be long before he shall put her away from him. Maybe he shall send her to the block."

"God help me," Cranmer said. "What a hellish scheme is this."

He pondered for a while, standing upright and fraily thrusting his hand into his bosom.

"You shall never get the King so to believe," he said; "this is an idle invention. I will none of it."

"Why, it may be done, I do believe," Lascelles said, "and greatly it shall help us."

"No, I will none of it," the Archbishop said. "It is a foul scheme. Besides, you must have many witnesses."

"I have some already," Lascelles said, "and when we come to London Town I shall have many more. It was not for nothing that the Great Privy Seal commended me."

"But to make the King," Cranmer uttered, as if he were aghast and amazed, "to make the King—this King who knoweth that his wife hath done no wrong—who knoweth it so well as tonight he hath proven— to make *him*, him, to put her away. . . why, the tiger is not so fell, nor the Egyptian worm preyeth not on its kind. This is an imagination so horrible—"

"Please it your Grace," Lascelles said softly, "what beast or brute hath your Grace ever seen to betray its kind as man will betray brother, son, father, or consort?"

The Archbishop raised his hands above his head.

"What lesser bull of the herd, or lesser ram, ever so played traitor to his leader as Brutus played to Cæsar Julius? And these be times less noble."

PART IV
THE END OF THE SONG

I

The Queen was at Hampton, and it was the late autumn. She had been sad since they came from Pontefract, for it had seemed more than ever apparent that the King's letter to Rome must be ever delayed in the sending. Daily, at night, the King swore with great oaths that the letter must be sent and his soul saved. He trembled to think that if then he died in his bed he must be eternally damned, and she added her persuasions, such as that each soul that died in his realms before that letter was sent went before the Throne of Mercy unshriven and unhouselled, so that their burden of souls grew very great. And in the midnights, the King would start up and cry that all was lost and himself accursed.

And it appeared that he and his house were accursed in these days, for when they were come back to Hampton, they found the small Prince Edward was very ill. He was swollen all over his little body, so that the doctors said it was a dropsy. But how, the King cried, could it be a dropsy in so young a child and one so grave and so nurtured and tended? Assuredly it must be some marvel wrought by the saints to punish him, or by the Fiend to tempt him. And so he would rave, and cast tremulous hands above his head. And he would say that God, to punish him, would have of him his dearest and best.

And when the Queen urged him, therefore, to make his peace with God, he would cry out that it was too late. God would make no peace with him. For if God were minded to have him at peace, wherefore would He not smoothe the way to this reconciliation with His vicegerent that sat at Rome in Peter's chair? There was no smoothing of that way—for every day there arose new difficulties and torments.

The King o' Scots would come into no alliance with him; the King of France would make no bid for the hand of his daughter Mary; it went ill with the Emperor in his fighting with the Princes of Almain and the Schmalkaldners, so that the Emperor would be of the less use as an ally against France and the Scots.

"Why!" he would cry to the Queen, "if God in His Heaven would have me make a peace with Rome, wherefore will He not give victory over a parcel of Lutheran knaves and swine? Wherefore will He not deliver into my hands these beggarly Scots and these atheists of France?"

At night the Queen would bring him round to vowing that first he would make peace with God and trust in His great mercy for a prosperous issue. But each morning he would be afraid for his sovereignty; a new letter would come from Norfolk, who had gone on an embassy to his French friends, believing fully that the King was minded to marry to one of them his daughter. But the French King was not ready to believe this. And the King's eyes grew red and enraged; he looked no man in the face, not even the Queen, but glanced aside into corners, uttered blasphemies, and said that he—he!—was the head of the Church and would have no overlord.

The Bishop Gardiner came up from his See in Winchester. But though he was the head of the Papist party in the realm, the Queen had little comfort in him. For he was a dark and masterful prelate, and never ceased to urge her to cast out Cranmer from his archbishopric and to give it to him. And with him the Lady Mary sided, for she would have Cranmer's head before all things, since Cranmer it was that most had injured her mother. Moreover, he was so incessant in his urging the King to make an alliance with the Catholic Emperor that at last, about the time that Norfolk came back from France, the King was mightily enraged, so that he struck the Bishop of Winchester in the face, and swore that his friend the Kaiser was a rotten plank, since he could not rid himself of a few small knaves of Lutheran princes.

Thus for long the Queen was sad; the little Prince very sick; and the King ate no food, but sat gazing at the victuals, though the Queen cooked some messes for him with her own hand.

ONE SUNDAY AFTER EVENSONG, AT which Cranmer himself had read prayers, the King came nearly merrily to his supper.

"Ho, chuck," he said, "you have your enemies. Here hath been Cranmer weeping to me with a parcel of tales writ on paper."

He offered it to her to read, but she would not; for, she said, she knew well that she had many enemies, only, very safely she could trust her fame in her Lord's hands.

"Why, you may," he said, and sat him down at the table to eat, with the paper stuck in his belt. "Body o' God!" he said. "If it had been any but Cranmer he had eaten bread in Hell this night. 'A wept and trembled! Body o' God! Body o' God!'"

And that night he was more merry before the fire than he had been for many weeks. He had in the music to play a song of his own writing, and afterwards he swore that next day he would ride to London, and then at his council send that which she would have sent to Rome.

"For, for sure," he said, "there is no peace in this world for me save when I hear you pray. And how shall you pray well for me save in the old form and fashion?"

He lolled back in his chair and gazed at her.

"Why," he said, "it is a proof of the great mercy of the Saviour that He sent you on earth in so fair a guise. For if you had not been so fair, assuredly I had not noticed you. Then would my soul have gone straightway to Hell."

And he called that the letter to Rome might be brought to him, and read it over in the firelight. He set it in his belt alongside the other paper, that next day when he came to London he might lay it in the hands of Sir Thomas Carter, that should carry it to Rome.

The Queen said: "Praise God!"

For though she was not set to believe that next day that letter would be sent, or for many days more, yet it seemed to her that by little and little she was winning him to her will.

II

Gardiner, Bishop of Winchester, had builded him a new tennis court in where his stables had been before poverty had caused him to sell the major part of his horseflesh. He called to him the Duke of Norfolk, who was of the Papist cause, and Sir Henry Wriothesley who was always betwixt and between, according as the cat jumped, to see this new building of his that was made of a roofed-in quadrangle where the stable doors were bricked up or barred to make the grille.

But though Norfolk and Wriothesley came very early in the afternoon, while it was yet light, to his house, they wasted most of the daylight hours in talking of things indifferent before they went to their inspection of this court. They stood talking in a long gallery beneath very high windows, and there were several chaplains and young priests and young gentlemen with them, and most of the talk was of a bear-baiting that there should be in Smithfield come Saturday. Sir Henry Wriothesley matched seven of his dogs against the seven best of the Duke's, that they should the longer hold to the bear once they were on him, and most of the young gentlemen wagered for Sir Henry's dogs that he had bred from a mastiff out of Portugal.

But when this talk had mostly died down, and when already twilight had long fallen, the Bishop said—

"Come, let us visit this new tennis place of mine. I think I shall show you somewhat that you have not before seen."

He bade, however, his gentlemen and priests to stay where they were, for they had all many times seen the court or building. When he led the way, prelatical and black, for the Duke and Wriothesley, into the lower corridors of his house, the priests and young gentlemen bowed behind his back, one at the other.

In the courtyard there were four hounds of a heavy and stocky breed that came bounding and baying all round them, so that it was only by vigilance that Gardiner could save Wriothesley's shins, for he was a man that all dogs and children hated.

"Sirs," the Bishop said, "these dogs that ye see and hear will let no man but me—not even my grooms or stablemen—pass this yard. I have bred them to that so I may be secret when I will."

He set the key in the door that was in the bottom wall of the court. "There is no other door here save that which goes into the stable where the grille is. There I have a door to enter and fetch out the balls that pass there."

In the court itself it was absolute blackness.

"I trow we may talk very well without lights," he said. "Come into this far corner."

Yet, though there was no fear of being overheard, each of these three stole almost on tiptoe and held his breath, and in the dark and shadowy place they made a more dark and more shadowy patch with their heads all close together.

Suddenly it was as if the Bishop dropped the veil that covered his passions.

"I may well build tennis courts," he said, and his voice had a ring of wild and malignant passion. "I may well build courts for tennis play. Nothing else is left for me to do."

In the blackness no word came from his listeners.

"You too may do the like," the Bishop said. "But I would you do it quickly, for soon neither the one nor the other of you but will be stripped so bare that you shall not have enough to buy balls with."

The Duke made an impatient sound like a drawing in of his breath, but still he spoke no word.

"I tell you, both of you," the Bishop's voice came, "that all of us have been fooled. Who was it that helped to set on high this one that now presses us down? I did! I! . . .

"It was I that called the masque at my house where first the King did see her. It was I that advised her how to bear herself. And what gratitude has been shown me? I have been sent to sequester myself in my see; I have been set to gnaw my fingers as they had been old bones thrown to a dog. Truly, no juicy meats have been my share. Yet it was I set this woman where she sits. . ."

"I too have my griefs," the Duke of Norfolk's voice came.

"And I, God wot," came Wriothesley's.

"Why, you have been fooled," Gardiner's voice; "and well you know it. For who was it that sent you both, one after the other, into France thinking that you might make a match between the Lady Royal and the Duke of Orleans?—Who but the Queen?—For well she knew that ye loved the French and their King as they had been your brothers. And well we know now that never in the mind of her, nor in that of the King whom she bewitches and enslaves, was there any thought save that the Lady Royal should be wedded to Spain. So ye are fooled."

He let his voice sink low; then he raised it again—

"Fooled! Fooled! Fooled! You two and I. For who of your friends the French shall ever believe again word that you utter. And all your goods and lands this Queen will have for the Church, so that she may have utter power with a parcel of new shavelings, that will not withstand her. So all the land will come in to her leash... We are fooled and ruined, ye and I alike."

"Well, we know this," the Duke's voice said distastefully. "You have no need to rehearse griefs that too well we feel. There is no lord, either of our part or of the other, that would not have her down."

"But what will ye do?" Gardiner said.

"Nothing may we do!" the voice of Wriothesley with its dismal terror came to their ears. "The King is too firmly her Highness's man."

"Her 'Highness,'" the Bishop mocked him with a bitter scorn. "I believe you would yet curry favour with this Queen of straw."

"It is a man's province to be favourable in the eyes of his Prince," the buried voice came again. "If I could win her favour I would. But well ye know there is no way."

"Ye ha' mingled too much with Lutheran swine," the Bishop said. "Now it is too late for you."

"So it is," Wriothesley said. "I think you, Bishop, would have done it too had you been able to make your account of it."

The Bishop snarled invisibly.

But the voice of Norfolk came malignantly upon them.

"This is all of a piece with your silly schemings. Did I come here to hear ye wrangle? It is peril enow to come here. What will ye do?"

"I will make a pact with him of the other side?" the Bishop said.

"Misery!" the Duke said; "did I come here to hear this madness? You and Cranmer have sought each other's heads this ten years. Will you seek his aid now? What may he do? He is as rotten a reed as thou or Wriothesley."

The Bishop cried suddenly with a loud voice—

"Ho, there! Come you out!"

Norfolk set his hand to his sword and so did Wriothesley. It was in both their minds, as it were one thought, that if this was a treason of the Bishop's he should there die.

From the blackness of the wall sides where the grille was there came the sound of a terroring lock and a creaking door.

"God!" Norfolk said; "who is this?"

There came the sound of breathing of one man who walked with noiseless shoes.

"Have you heard enow to make you believe that these lords' hearts are true to the endeavour of casting the Queen down?"

"I have heard enow," a smooth voice said. "I never thought it had been otherwise."

"Who is this?" Wriothesley said. "I will know who this is that has heard us."

"You fool," Gardiner said; "this man is of the other side."

"They have come to you!" Norfolk said.

"To whom else should we come," the voice answered.

A subtler silence of agitation and thought was between these two men. At last Gardiner said—

"Tell these lords what you would have of us?"

"We would have these promises," the voice said; "first, of you, my Lord Duke, that if by our endeavours your brother's child be brought to a trial for unchastity you will in no wise aid her at that trial with your voice or your encouragement."

"A trial!" and "Unchastity!" the Duke said. "This is a winter madness. Ye know that my niece—St Kevin curse her for it—is as chaste as the snow."

"So was your other niece, Anne Boleyn, for all you knew, yet you dogged her to death," Gardiner said. "Then you plotted with Papists; now it is the turn of the Lutherans. It is all one, so we are rid of this pest."

"Well, I will promise it," the Duke said. "Ye knew I would. It was not worth while to ask me."

"Secondly," the voice said, "of you, my Lord Duke, we would have this service: that you should swear your niece is a much older woman than she looks. Say, for instance, that she was in truth not the eleventh but the second child of your brother Edmund. Say that, out of vanity, to make herself seem more forward with the learned tongues when she was a child, she would call herself her younger sister that died in childbed."

"But wherefore?" the Duke said.

"Why," Gardiner answered, "this is a very subtle scheme of this gentleman's devising. He will prove against her certain lewdnesses when she was a child in your mother's house. If then she was a child of ten or so, knowing not evil from good, this might not undo her. But if you can make her seem then eighteen or twenty it will be enough to hang her."

Norfolk reflected.

"Well, I will say I heard that of her age," he said; "but ye had best get nurses and women to swear to these things."

"We have them now," the voice said. "And it will suffice if your Grace will say that you heard these things of old of your brother. For your Grace will judge this woman."

"Very willingly I will," Norfolk said; "for if I do not soon, she will utterly undo both me and all my friends."

He reflected again.

"Those things will I do and more yet, if you will."

"Why, that will suffice," the voice said. It took a new tone in the darkness.

"Now for you, Sir Henry Wriothesley," it said. "These simple things you shall promise. Firstly, since you have the ear of the Mayor of London you shall advise him in no way to hinder certain meetings of Lutherans that I shall tell you of later. And, though it is your province so to do, you shall in no wise hinder a certain master printer from printing what broadsides and libels he will against the Queen. For it is essential, if this project is to grow and flourish, that it shall be spread abroad that the Queen did bewitch the King to her will on that night at Pontefract that you remember, when she had her cousin in her bedroom. So broadsides shall be made alleging that by sorcery she induced the King to countenance his own shame. And we have witnesses to swear that it was by appointment, not by chance, that she met with Culpepper upon the moorside. But all that we will have of you is that you will promise these two things—that the Lutherans may hold certain meetings and the broadsides be printed."

"Those I will promise," came in Wriothesley's buried voice.

"Then I will no more of you," the other's words came. They heard his hands feeling along the wall till he came to the door by which he had entered. The Bishop followed him, to let him out by a little door he had had opened for that one night, into the street.

When he came back to the other two and unfolded to them what was the scheme of the Archbishop's man, they agreed that it was a very good plan. Then they fell to considering whether it should not serve their turn to betray this plan at once to the Queen. But they agreed that, if they preserved the Queen, they would be utterly ruined, as they were like to be now, whereas, if it succeeded, they would be much the better off. And, even if it failed, they lost nothing, for it would not readily be believed that they had aided Lutherans, and there were no letters or writings.

So they agreed to abide honourably by their promises—and very certain they were that if clamour enough could be raised against the Queen, the King would be bound into putting her away, though it were against his will.

III

In the Master Printer Badge's house—and he was the uncle of Margot and of the young Poins—there was a great and solemn dissertation towards. For word had been brought that certain strangers come on an embassy from the Duke of Cleves were minded to hear how the citizens of London—or at any rate those of them that held German doctrines—bore themselves towards Schmalkaldnerism and the doctrines of Luther.

It was understood that these strangers were of very high degree—of a degree so high that they might scarce be spoken to by the meaner sort. And for many days messengers had been going between the house of the Archbishop at Lambeth and that of the Master Printer, to school him how this meeting must be conducted.

His old father was by that time dead—having died shortly after his granddaughter Margot had been put away from the Queen's Court—so that the house-place was clear. And of all the old furnishings none remained. There were presses all round the wall, and lockers for men to sit upon. The table had been cleared away into the printer's chapel; a lectern stood a-midmost of the room, and before the hearth-place, in the very ingle, there was set the great chair in which aforetimes the old man had sat so long.

Early that evening, though already it was dusk, the body of citizens were assembled. Most of them had haggard faces, for the times were evil for men of their persuasion, and nearly all of them were draped in black after the German fashion among Lutherans of that day. They ranged themselves on the lockers along the wall, and with set faces, in a funereal row, they awaited the coming of this great stranger. There were no Germans amongst them, for so, it was given out, he would have it—either because he would not be known by name or for some other reason.

The Master Printer, in the pride of his craft, wore his apron. He stood in the centre of the room facing the hearth-place; his huge arms were bare—for bare-armed he always worked—his black beard was knotted into little curls, his face was so broad that you hardly remarked that his nose was hooked like an owl's beak. And about the man there was an air of sombreness and mystery. He had certain papers on his lectern, and several sheets of the great Bible that he was then printing by the Archbishop's license and command. They sang all together and with loud voices the canticle called "A Refuge fast is God the Lord."

Then, with huge gestures of his hands, he uttered the words—

"This is the very word of God," and began to read from the pages of his Bible. He read first the story of David and Saul, his great voice trembling with ecstasy.

"This David is our King," he said. "This Saul that he slew is the Beast of Rome. The Solomon that cometh after shall be the gracious princeling that ye wot of, for already he is wise beyond his years and beyond most grown men."

The citizens around the walls cried "Amen." And because the strangers tarried to come, he called to his journeymen that stood in the inner doorway to bring him the sheets of the Bible whereon he had printed the story of Ehud and Eglon.

"This king that ye shall hear of as being slain," he cried out, "is that foul bird the Kaiser Carl, that harries the faithful in Almain. This good man that shall slay him is some German lord. Who he shall be we know not yet; maybe it shall be this very stranger that tonight shall sit to hear us."

His brethren muttered a low, deep, and uniform prayer that soon, soon the Lord should send them this boon.

But he had not got beyond the eleventh verse of this history before there came from without a sound of trumpets, and through the windows the light of torches and the scarlet of the guard that, it was said, the King had sent to do honour to this stranger.

"Come in, be ye who ye may!" the printer cried to the knockers at his door.

There entered the hugest masked man that they ever had seen. All in black he was, and horrifying and portentous he strode in. His sleeves and shoulders were ballooned after the German fashion, his sword clanked on the tiles. He was a vision of black, for his mask that appeared as big as another man's garment covered all his face, though they could see he had a grey beard when sitting down. He gazed at the fire askance.

He said—his voice was heavy and husky—

"*Gruesset Gott*," and those of the citizens that had painfully attained to so much of that tongue answered him with—

"*Lobet den Herr im Himmels Reich!*"

He had with him one older man that wore a half-mask, and was trembling and clean-shaven, and one younger, that was English, to act as interpreter when it was needed. He was clean-shaven, too, and in the English habit he appeared thin and tenuous. They said he was a gentleman of the Archbishop's, and that his name was Lascelles.

He opened the meeting with saying that these great strangers were come from beyond the seas, and would hear answers to certain questions. He took a paper from his pouch and said that, in order that he might stick to the points that these strangers would know of, he had written down those questions on that paper.

"How say ye, masters?" he finished. "Will ye give answers to these questions truly, and of your knowledge?"

"Aye will we," the printer said, "for to that end we are gathered here. Is it not so, my masters?"

And the assembly answered—

"Aye, so it is."

Lascelles read from his paper:

"How is it with this realm of England?"

The printer glanced at the paper that was upon his lectern. He made answer—

"Well! But not over well!"

And at these words Lascelles feigned surprise, lifting his well-shapen and white hand in the air.

"How is this that ye say?" he uttered. "Are ye all of this tale?"

A deep "Aye!" came from all these chests. There was one old man that could never keep still. He had huge limbs, a great ruffled poll of grizzling hair, and his legs that were in jerkins of red leather kicked continuously in little convulsions. He peered every minute at some new thing, very closely, holding first his tablets so near that he could see only with one eye, then the whistle that hung round his neck, then a little piece of paper that he took from his poke. He cried out in a deep voice—"Aye! aye! Not over well. Witchcraft and foul weather and rocks, my mates and masters all!" so that he appeared to be a seaman—and indeed he traded to the port of Antwerp, in the Low Countries, where he had learned of some of the Faith.

"Why," Lascelles said, "be ye not contented with our goodly King?"

"Never was a better since Solomon ruled in Jewry," the shipman cried out.

"Is it, then, the Lords of the King's Council that ye are discontented with?"

"Nay, they are goodly men, for they are of the King's choosing," one answered—a little man with a black pill-hat.

"Why, speak through your leader," the stranger said heavily from the hearth-place. "Here is too much skimble-skamble." The old man beside him leaned over his chair-back and whispered in his ear. But the stranger shook his head heavily. He sat and gazed at the brands. His great hands were upon his knees, pressed down, but now and again they moved as if he were in some agony.

"It is well that ye do as the Lord commandeth," Lascelles said; "for in Almain, whence he cometh, there is wont to be a great order and observance." He held his paper up again to the light. "Master Printer, answer now to this question: Find ye aught amiss with the judges and justices of this realm?"

"Nay; they do judge indifferent well betwixt cause and cause," the printer answered from his paper.

"Or with the serjeants, the apparitors, the collectors of taxes, or the Parliament men?"

"These, too, perform indifferent well their appointed tasks," the printer said gloomily.

"Or is it with the Church of this realm that ye find fault?"

"Body of God!" the stranger said heavily.

"Nay!" the printer answered, "for the supreme head of that Church is the King, a man learned before all others in the law of God; such a King as speaketh as though he were that mouthpiece of the Most High that the Antichrist at Rome claimeth to be."

"Is it, then, with the worshipful the little Prince of Wales that ye are discontented?" Lascelles read, and the printer answered that there was not such another Prince of his years for promise and for performance, too, in all Christendom.

The stranger said from the hearth-place—

"Well! we are commended," and his voice was bitter and ironical.

"How is it, then," Lascelles read on, "that ye say all is not over well in the land?"

The printer's gloomy and black features glared with a sudden rage.

"How should all be well with a land," he cried, "where in high places reigns harlotry?" He raised his clenched fist on high and glared round upon his audience. "Corruption that reacheth round and about and down till it hath found a seedbed even in this poor house of my father's? Or if it is well with this land now, how shall it continue well when witchcraft rules near the King himself, and the Devil of Rome hath there his emissaries."

A chitter of sound came from his audience, so that it appeared that they were all of a strain. They moved in their seats; the shipman cried out—

"Ay! witchcraft! witchcraft!"

The huge bulk of the stranger, black and like a bull's, half rose from its chair.

"Body of God!" he cried out. "This I will not bear."

Again the older man leaned solicitously above him and whispered, pleading with his hands, and Lascelles said hastily—

"Speak of your own knowledge. How should you know of what passes in high places?"

"Why!" the printer cried out, "is it not the common report? Do not all men know it? Do not the butchers sing of it in the shambles, and the bot-flies buzz of it one to the other? I tell you it is spread from here into Almain, where the very horse-sellers are a-buzz with it."

In his chair the stranger cried out—

"Ah! ah!" as if he were in great pain. He struggled with his feet and then sat still.

"I have heard witnesses that will testify to these things," the printer said. "I will bring them here into this room before ye." He turned upon the stranger. "Master," he said, "if ye know not of this, you are the only man in England that is ignorant!"

The stranger said with a bitter despair—

"Well, I am come to hear what ye do say!"

So he heard tales from all the sewers of London, and it was plain to him that all the commonalty cried shame upon their King. He screamed and twisted there in his chair at the last, and when he was come out into the darkness he fell upon his companion, and beat him so that he screamed out.

He might have died—for, though the King's guard with their torches and halberds were within a bowshot of them, they stirred no limb. And it was a party of fellows bat-fowling along the hedges of that field that came through the dark, attracted by the glare of the torches, the blaze of the scarlet clothes, and the outcry.

And when they came, asking why that great man belaboured this thin and fragile one, black shadows both against the light, the big man answered, howling—

"This man hath made me bounden to slay my wife."

They said that that was a thing some of them would have been glad of.

But the great figure cast itself on the ground at the foot of a tree that stretched up like nerves and tentacles into the black sky. He tore the wet earth with his fingers, and the men stood round him till the Duke of Norfolk, coming with his sword drawn, hunted them afar off, and they fell again to beating the hedges to drive small birds into their nets.

For, they said, these were evidently of the quality whose griefs were none of theirs.

IV

The Queen was walking in the long gallery of Hampton Court. The afternoon was still new, but rain was falling very fast, so that through the windows all trees were blurred with mist, and all alleys ran with water, and it was very grey in the gallery. The Lady Mary was with her, and sat in a window-seat reading in a book. The Queen, as she walked, was netting a silken purse of a purple colour; her gown was very richly embroidered of gold thread worked into black velvet, and the heavy day pressed heavily on her senses, so that she sought that silence more willingly. For three days she had had no news of her lord, but that morning he was come back to Hampton, though she had not yet seen him, for it was ever his custom to put off all work of the day before he came to the Queen. Thus, if she were sad, she was tranquil; and, considering only that her work of bringing him to God must begin again that night, she let her thoughts rest upon the netting of her purse. The King, she had heard, was with his council. Her uncle was come to Court, and Gardiner of Winchester, and Cranmer of Canterbury, along with Sir A. Wriothesley, and many other lords, so that she augured it would be a very full council, and that night there would be a great banquet if she was not mistaken.

She remembered that it was now many months since she had been shown for Queen from that very gallery in the window that opened upon the Cardinal's garden. The King had led her by the hand. There had been a great crying out of many people of the lower sort that crowded the terrace before the garden. Now the rain fell, and all was desolation. A yeoman in brown fustian ran bending his head before the tempestuous rain. A rook, blown impotently backwards, essayed slowly to cross towards the western trees. Her eyes followed him until a great gust blew him in a wider curve, backwards and up, and when again he steadied himself he was no more than a blot on the wet greyness of the heavens.

There was an outcry at the door, and a woman ran in. She was crying out still: she was all in grey, with the white coif of the Queen's service. She fell down upon her knees, her hands held out.

"Pardon!" she cried. "Pardon! Let not my brother come in. He prowls at the door."

It was Mary Hall, she that had been Mary Lascelles. The Queen came over to raise her up, and to ask what it was she sought. But the woman wept so loud, and so continually cried out that her brother was the fiend incarnate, that the Queen could ask no questions. The Lady Mary looked up over her book without stirring her body. Her eyes were awakened and sardonic.

The waiting-maid looked affrightedly over her shoulders at the door.

"Well, your brother shall not come in here," the Queen said. "What would he have done to you?"

"Pardon!" the woman cried out. "Pardon!"

"Why, tell me of your fault," the Queen said.

"I have given false witness!" Mary Hall blubbered out. "I would not do it. But you do not know how they confuse a body. And they threaten with cords and thumbscrews." She shuddered with her whole body. "Pardon!" she cried out. "Pardon!"

And then suddenly she poured forth a babble of lamentations, wringing her hands, and rubbing her lips together. She was a woman passed of thirty, but thin still and fair like her brother in the face, for she was his twin.

"Ah," she cried, "he threated that if I would not give evidence I must go back to Lincolnshire. You do not know what it is to go back to Lincolnshire. Ah, God! the old father, the old house, the wet. My clothes were all mouldered. I was willing to give true evidence to save myself, but they twisted it to false. It was the Duke of Norfolk. . ."

The Lady Mary came slowly over the floor.

"Against whom did you give your evidence?" she said, and her voice was cold, hard, and commanding.

Mary Hall covered her face with her hands, and wailed desolately in a high note, like a wolf's howl, that reverberated in that dim gallery.

The Lady Mary struck her a hard blow with the cover of her book upon the hands and the side of her head.

"Against whom did you give your evidence?" she said again.

The woman fell over upon one hand, the other she raised to shield herself. Her eyes were flooded with great teardrops; her mouth was open in an agony. The Lady Mary raised her book to strike again: its covers were of wood, and its angles bound with silver work. The woman screamed out, and then uttered—

"Against Dearham and one Mopock first. And then against Sir T. Culpepper."

The Queen stood up to her height; her hand went over her heart; the netted purse dropped to the floor soundlessly.

"God help me!" Mary Hall cried out. "Dearham and Culpepper are both dead!"

The Queen sprang back three paces.

"How dead!" she cried. "They were not even ill."

"Upon the block," the maid said. "Last night, in the dark, in their gaols."

The Queen let her hands fall slowly to her sides.

"Who did this?" she said, and Mary Hall answered—

"It was the King!"

The Lady Mary set her book under her arm.

"Ye might have known it was the King," she said harshly. The Queen was as still as a pillar of ebony and ivory, so black her dress was, and so white her face and pendant hands.

"I repent me! I repent me!" the maid cried out. "When I heard that they were dead I repented me and came here. The old Duchess of Norfolk is in gaol: she burned the letters of Dearham! The Lady Rochford is in gaol, and old Sir Nicholas, and the Lady Cicely that was ever with the Queen; the Lord Edmund Howard shall to gaol and his lady."

"Why," the Lady Mary said to the Queen, "if you had not had such a fear of nepotism, your father and mother and grandmother and cousin had been here about you, and not so easily taken."

The Queen stood still whilst all her hopes fell down.

"They have taken Lady Cicely that was ever with me," she said.

"It was the Duke of Norfolk that pressed me most," Mary Lascelles cried out.

"Aye, he would," the Lady Mary answered.

The Queen tottered upon her feet.

"Ask her more," she said. "I will not speak with her."

"The King in his council. . ." the girl began.

"Is the King in his council upon these matters?" the Lady Mary asked.

"Aye, he sitteth there," Mary Hall said. "And he hath heard evidence of Mary Trelyon the Queen's maid, how that the Queen's Highness did bid her begone on the night that Sir T. Culpepper came to her room, before he came. And how that the Queen was very insistent that she should go, upon the score of fatigue and the lateness of the hour. And she hath deponed that on other nights, too, this has happened, that the

Queen's Highness, when she hath come late to bed, hath equally done the same thing. And other her maids have deponed how the Queen hath sent them from her presence and relieved them of tasks—"

"Well, well," the Lady Mary said, "often I have urged the Queen that she should be less gracious. Better it had been if she had beat ye all as I have done; then had ye feared to betray her."

"Aye," Mary Hall said, "it is a true thing that your Grace saith there."

"Call me not your Grace," the Lady Mary said. "I will be no Grace in this court of wolves and hogs."

That was the sole thing that she said to show she was of the Queen's party. But ever she questioned the kneeling woman to know what evidence had been given, and of the attitude of the lords.

The young Poins had sworn roundly that the Queen had bidden him to summon no guards when her cousin had broken in upon her. Only Udal had said that he knew nothing of how Katharine had agreed with her cousin whilst they were in Lincolnshire. It had been after his time there that Culpepper came. It had been after his time, too, and whilst he lay in chains at Pontefract that Culpepper had come to her door. He stuck to that tale, though the Duke of Norfolk had beat and threatened him never so.

"Why, what wolves Howards be," the Lady Mary said, "for it is only wolves, of all beasts, that will prey upon the sick of their kind."

The Queen stood there, swaying back as if she were very sick, her eyes fast closed, and the lids over them very blue.

It was only when the Lady Mary drew from the woman an account of the King's demeanour that she showed a sign of hearing.

"His Highness," the woman said, "sate always mute."

"His Highness would," the Lady Mary said. "He is in that at least royal—that he letteth jackals do his hunting."

It was only when the Archbishop of Canterbury, reading from the indictment of Culpepper, had uttered the words: "did by the obtaining of the Lady Rochford meet with the Queen's Highness by night in a secret and vile place," that the King had called out—

"Body of God! mine own bedchamber!" as if he were hatefully mocking the Archbishop.

The Queen leant suddenly forward—

"Said he no more than that?" she cried eagerly.

"No more, oh your dear Grace," the maid said. And the Queen shuddered and whispered—

"No more!—And I have spoken to this woman to obtain no more than 'no more.'"

Again she closed her eyes, and she did not again speak, but hung her head forward as if she were thinking.

"Heaven help me!" the maid said.

"Why, think no more of Heaven," the Lady Mary said, "there is but the fire of hell for such beasts as you."

"Had you such a brother as mine—" Mary Hall began. But the Lady Mary cried out—

"Cease, dog! I have a worse father, but you have not found him force me to work vileness."

"All the other Papists have done worse than I," Mary Hall said, "for they it was that forced us by threats to speak."

"Not one was of the Queen's side?" the Lady Mary said.

"Not one," Mary Hall answered. "Gardiner was more fierce against her than he of Canterbury, the Duke of Norfolk than either."

The Lady Mary said—

"Well! well!"

"Myself I did hear the Duke of Norfolk say, when I was drawn to give evidence, that he begged the King to let him tear my secrets from my heart. For so did he abhor the abominable deeds done by his two nieces, Anne Boleyn and Katharine Howard, that he could no longer desire to live. And he said neither could he live longer without some comfortable assurance of His Highness's royal favour. And so he fell upon me—"

The woman fell to silence. Without, the rain had ceased, and, like heavy curtains trailing near the ground, the clouds began to part and sweep away. A horn sounded, and there went a party of men with pikes across the terrace.

"Well, and what said you?" the Lady Mary said.

"Ask me not," Mary Lascelles said woefully. She averted her eyes to the floor at her side.

"By God, but I will know," the Lady Mary snarled. "You shall tell me." She had that of royal bearing from her sire that the woman was amazed at her words, and, awakening like one in a dream, she rehearsed the evidence that had been threated from her.

She had told of the lascivious revels and partings, in the maid's garret at the old Duchess's, when Katharine had been a child there. She had told how Marnock the musicker had called her his mistress, and how Dearham, Katharine's cousin, had beaten him. And how Dearham had given Katharine a half of a silver coin.

"Well, that is all true," the Lady Mary said. "How did you perjure yourself?"

"In the matter of the Queen's age," the woman faltered.

"How that?" the Lady Mary asked.

"The Duke would have me say that she was more than a young child."

The Lady Mary said, "Ah! ah! there is the yellow dog!" She thought for a moment.

"And you said?" she asked at last.

"The Duke threated me and threated me. And say I, 'Your Grace must know how young she was.' And says he, 'I would swear that at that date she was no child, but that I do not know how many of these nauseous Howard brats there be. Nor yet the order in which they came. But this I will swear that I think there has been some change of the Queen with a whelp that died in the litter, that she might seem more young. And of a surety she was always learned beyond her assumed years, so that it was not to be believed.'"

Mary Lascelles closed her eyes and appeared about to faint.

"Speak on, dog," Mary said.

The woman roused herself to say with a solemn piteousness—

"This I swear that before this trial, when my brother pressed me and threated me thus to perjure myself, I abhorred it and spat in his face. There was none more firm—nor one half so firm as I—against him. But oh, the Duke and the terror—and to be in a ring of so many villainous men. . ."

"So that you swore that the Queen's Highness, to your knowledge, was older than a child," the Lady Mary pressed her.

"Ay; they would have me say that it was she that commanded to have these revels. . ."

She leaned forward with both her hands on the floor, in the attitude of a beast that goes four-footed. She cried out—

"Ask me no more! ask me no more!"

"Tell! tell! Beast!" the Lady Mary said.

"They threated me with torture," the woman panted. "I could do no less. I heard Margot Poins scream."

"They have tortured her?" the Lady Mary said.

"Ay, and she was in her pains elsewise," the woman said.

"Did she say aught?" the Lady Mary said.

"No! no!" the woman panted. Her hair had fallen loose in her coif, it depended on to her shoulder.

"Tell on! tell on!" the Lady Mary said.

"They tortured her, and she did not say one word more, but ever in her agony cried out, 'Virtuous! virtuous!' till her senses went."

Mary Hall again raised herself to her knees.

"Let me go, let me go," she moaned. "I will not speak before the Queen. I had been as loyal as Margot Poins. . . But I will not speak before the Queen. I love her as well as Margot Poins. But. . . I will not—"

She cried out as the Lady Mary struck her, and her face was lamentable with its opened mouth. She scrambled to one knee; she got on both, and ran to the door. But there she cried out—

"My brother!" and fell against the wall. Her eyes were fixed upon the Lady Mary with a baleful despair, she gasped and panted for breath.

"It is upon you if I speak," she said. "Merciful God, do not bid me speak before the Queen!"

She held out her hands as if she had been praying.

"Have I not proved that I loved this Queen?" she said. "Have I not fled here to warn her? Is it not my life that I risk? Merciful God! Merciful God! Bid me not to speak."

"Speak!" the Lady Mary said.

The woman appealed to the Queen with her eyes streaming, but Katharine stood silent and like a statue with sightless eyes. Her lips smiled, for she thought of her Redeemer; for this woman she had neither ears nor eyes.

"Speak!" the Lady Mary said.

"God help you, be it on your head," the woman cried out, "that I speak before the Queen. It was the King that bade me say she was so old. I would not say it before the Queen, but you have made me!"

The Lady Mary's hands fell powerless to her sides, the book from her opened fingers jarred on the hard floor.

"Merciful God!" she said. "Have I such a father?"

"It was the King!" the woman said. "His Highness came to life when he heard these words of the Duke's, that the Queen was older than she reported. He would have me say that the Queen's Highness was of a marriageable age and contracted to her cousin Dearham."

"Merciful God!" the Lady Mary said again. "Dear God, show me some way to tear from myself the sin of my begetting. I had rather my mother's confessor had been my father than the King! Merciful God!"

"Never was woman pressed as I was to say this thing. And well ye wot—better than I did before—what this King is. I tell you—and I swear it—"

She stopped and trembled, her eyes, from which the colour had gone, wide open and lustreless, her face pallid and ashen, her mouth hanging open. The Queen was moving towards her.

She came very slowly, her hands waving as if she sought support from the air, but her head was erect.

"What will you do?" the Lady Mary said. "Let us take counsel!"

Katharine Howard said no word. It was as if she walked in her sleep.

V

The King sat on the raised throne of his council chamber. All the Lords of his Council were there and all in black. There was Norfolk with his yellow face who feigned to laugh and scoff, now that he had proved himself no lover of the Queen's. There was Gardiner of Winchester, sitting forward with his cruel and eager eyes upon the table. Next him was the Lord Mayor, Michael Dormer, and the Lord Chancellor. And so round the horse-shoe table against the wall sat all the other lords and commissioners that had been appointed to make inquiry. Sir Anthony Browne was there, and Wriothesley with his great beard, and the Duke of Suffolk with his hanging jaw. A silence had fallen upon them all, and the witnesses were all done with.

On high on his throne the King sat, monstrous and leaning over to one side, his face dabbled with tears. He gazed upon Cranmer who stood on high beside him, the King gazing upwards into his face as if for comfort and counsel.

"Why, you shall save her for me?" he said.

Cranmer's face was haggard, and upon it too there were tears.

"It were the gladdest thing that ever I did," he said, "for I do believe this Queen is not so guilty."

"God of His mercy bless thee, Cranmer," he said, and wearily he touched his black bonnet at the sacred name. "I have done all that I might when I spoke with Mary Hall. It shall save me her life."

Cranmer looked round upon the lords below them; they were all silent but only the Duke of Norfolk who laughed to the Lord Mayor. The Lord Mayor, a burly man, was more pallid and haggard than any. All the others had fear for themselves written upon their faces. But the citizen was not used to these trials, of which the others had seen so many.

The Archbishop fell on his knees on the step before the King's throne.

"Gracious and dread Lord," he said, and his low voice trembled like that of a schoolboy, "Saviour, Lord, and Fount of Justice of this realm! Hitherto these trials have been of traitor-felons and villains outside the circle of your house. Now that they be judged and dead, we, your lords, pray you that you put off from you this most heavy task of judge. For inasmuch as we live by your life and have health by your health, in this realm afflicted with many sores that you alone can heal and dangers that you alone can ward off, so we have it assured and certain that many too great labours and matters laid upon you imperil us all. In that, as well for our selfish fears as for the great love, self-forgetting, that we have of your person, we pray you that—coming now to the trial of this your wife—you do rest, though well assured we are that greatly and courageously you would adventure it, upon the love of us your lords. Appoint, therefore, such a Commission as you shall well approve to make this most heavy essay and trial."

So low was his voice that, to hear him, many lords rose from their seats and came over against the throne. Thus all that company were in the upper part of the hall, and through the great window at the further end the sun shone down upon them, having parted the watery clouds. To their mass of black it gave blots and gouts of purple and blue and scarlet, coming through the dight panes.

"Lay off this burden of trial and examination upon us that so willingly, though with sighs and groans, would bear it."

Suddenly the King stood up and pointed, his jaw fallen open. Katharine Howard was coming up the floor of the hall. Her hands were folded before her; her face was rigid and calm; she looked neither to right nor to left, but only upon the King's face. At the edge of the sunlight she halted, so that she stood, a black figure in the bluish and stony gloom of the hall with the high roof a great way above her head. All the lords began to pull off their bonnets, only Norfolk said that he would not uncover before a harlot.

The Queen, looking upon Henry's face, said with icy and cold tones—

"I would have you to cease this torturing of witnesses. I will make confession."

No man then had a word to say. Norfolk had no word either.

"If you will have me confess to heresy, I will confess to heresy; if to treason, to treason. If you will have me confess to adultery, God help me and all of you, I will confess to adultery and all such sins."

The King cried out—

"No! no!" like a beast that is stabbed to the heart; but with cold eyes the Queen looked back at him.

"If you will have it adultery before marriage, it shall be so. If it be to be falseness to my Lord's bed, it shall be so; if it be both, in the name of God, be it both, and where you will and how. If you will have it spoken, here I speak it. If you will have it written, I will write out such words as you shall bid me write. I pray you leave my poor women be, especially them that be sick, for there are none that do not love me, and I do think that my death is all that you need."

She paused; there was no sound in the hall but the strenuous panting of the King.

"But whether," she said, "you shall believe this confession of mine, I leave to you that very well do know my conversation and my manner of life."

Again she paused and said—

"I have spoken. To it I will add that heartily I do thank my sovereign lord that raised me up. And, in public, I do say it, that he hath dealt justly by me. I pray you pardon me for having delayed thus long your labours. I will get me gone."

Then she dropped her eyes to the ground.

Again the King cried out—

"No! no!" and, stumbling to his feet he rushed down upon his courtiers and round the table. He came upon her before she was at the distant door.

"You shall not go!" he said. "Unsay! unsay!"

She said, "Ah!" and recoiled before him with an obdurate and calm repulsion.

"Get ye gone, all you minions and hounds," he cried. And running in upon them he assailed them with huge blows and curses, sobbing lamentably, so that they fled up the steps and out on to the rooms behind the throne. He came sobbing, swift and maddened, panting and crying out, back to where she awaited him.

"Unsay! unsay!" he cried out.

She stood calmly.

"Never will I unsay," she said. "For it is right that such a King as thou should be punished, and I do believe this: that there can no agony come upon you such as shall come if you do believe me false to you."

The coloured sunlight fell upon his face just down to the chin; his eyes glared horribly. She confronted him, being in the shadow. High up above them, painted and moulded angels soared on the roof with golden wings. He clutched at his throat.

"I do not believe it," he cried out.

"Then," she said, "I believe that it shall be only a second greater agony to you: for you shall have done me to death believing me guiltless."

A great motion of despair went over his whole body.

"Kat!" he said; "Body of God, Kat! I would not have you done to death. I have saved your life from your enemies."

She made him no answer, and he protested desperately—

"All this afternoon I have wrestled with a woman to make her say that you are older than your age, and precontracted to a cousin of yours. I have made her say it at last, so your life is saved."

She turned half to go from him, but he ran round in front of her.

"Your life is saved!" he said desperately, "for if you were precontracted to Dearham your marriage with me is void. And if your marriage with me is void, though it be proved against you that you were false to me, yet it is not treason, for you are not my wife."

Again she moved to circumvent him, and again he came before her.

"Speak!" he said, "speak!" But she folded her lips close. He cast his arms abroad in a passion of despair. "You shall be put away into a castle where you shall have such state as never empress had yet. All your will I will do. Always I will live near you in secret fashion."

"I will not be your leman," she said.

"But once you offered it!" he answered.

"Then you appeared in the guise of a king!" she said.

He withered beneath her tone.

"All you would have you shall have," he said. "I will call in a messenger and here and now send the letter that you wot of to Rome."

"Your Highness," she said, "I would not have the Church brought back to this land by one deemed an adult'ress. Assuredly, it should not prosper."

Again he sought to stay her going, holding out his arms to enfold her. She stepped back.

"Your Highness," she said, "I will speak some last words. And, as you know me well, you know that these irrevocably shall be my last to you!"

He cried—"Delay till you hear—"

"There shall be no delay," she said; "I will not hear." She smoothed a strand of hair that had fallen over her forehead in a gesture that she always had when she was deep in thoughts.

"This is what I would say," she uttered. And she began to speak levelly—

"Very truly you say when you say that once I made offer to be your leman. But it was when I was a young girl, mazed with reading of books in the learned tongue, and seeing all men as if they were men of those days. So you appeared to me such a man as was Pompey the Great, or as was Marius, or as was Sylla. For each of these great men erred; yet they erred greatly as rulers that would rule. Or rather I did see you such a one as was Cæsar Julius, who, as you well wot, crossed a Rubicon and set out upon a high endeavour. But you—never will you cross any Rubicon; always you blow hot in the evening and cold at dawn. Neither do you, as I had dreamed you did, rule in this your realm. For, even as a crow that just now I watched, you are blown hither and thither by every gust that blows. Now the wind of gossips blows so that you must have my life. And, before God, I am glad of it."

"Before God!" he cried out, "I would save you!"

"Aye," she answered sadly, "today you would save me; tomorrow a foul speech of one mine enemy shall gird you again to slay me. On the morrow you will repent, and on the morrow of that again you will repent of that. So you will balance and trim. If today you send a messenger to Rome, tomorrow you will send another, hastening by a shorter route, to stay him. And this I tell you, that I am not one to let my name be bandied for many days in the mouths of men. I had rather be called a sinner, adjudged and dead and forgotten. So I am glad that I am cast to die."

"You shall not die!" the King cried. "Body of God, you shall not die! I cannot live lacking thee. Kat—Kat—"

"Aye," she said, "I must die, for you are not such a one as can stay in the wind. Thus I tell you it will fall about that for many days you will waver, but one day you will cry out—Let her die this day! On the morrow of that day you will repent you, but, being dead, I shall be no more to be recalled to life. Why, man, with this confession of mine, heard by grooms and mayors of cities and the like, how shall you dare to save me? You know you shall not."

"And so, now I am cast for death, and I am very glad of it. For, if I had not so ensured and made it fated, I might later have wavered. For I am a weak woman, and strong men have taken dishonourable means to escape death when it came near. Now I am assured of death, and know that no means of yours can save me, nor no prayers nor yielding of mine. I came to you for that you might give this realm again to God. Now I see you will not—for not ever will you do it if it must abate you a jot of your sovereignty, and you never will do it without that abatement. So it is in vain that I have sinned.

"For I trow that I sinned in taking the crown from the woman that was late your wife. I would not have it, but you would, and I yielded. Yet it was a sin. Then I did a sin that good might ensue, and again I do it, and I hope that this sin that brings me down shall counterbalance that other that set me up. For well I know that to make this confession is a sin; but whether the one shall balance the other only the angels that are at the gates of Paradise shall assure me.

"In some sort I have done it for your Highness' sake—or, at least, that your Highness may profit in your fame thereby. For, though all that do know me will scarcely believe in it, the most part of men shall needs judge me by the reports that are set about. In the commonalty, and the princes of foreign courts, one may believe you justified of my blood, and, for this event, even to posterity your name shall be spared. I shall become such a little dust as will not fill a cup. Yet, at least, I shall not sully, in the eyes of men to come, your record.

"And that I am glad of; for this world is no place for me who am mazed by too much reading in old books. At first I would not believe it, though many have told me it was so. I was of the opinion that in the end right must win through. I think now that it never shall—or not for many ages—till our Saviour again come upon this earth with a great glory. But all this is a mystery of the great goodness of God and the temptations that do beset us poor mortality.

"So now I go! I think that you will not any more seek to hinder me, for you have heard how set I am on this course. I think, if I have done little good, I have done little harm, for I have sought to injure no man—though through me you have wracked some of my poor servants and slain my poor simple cousin. But that is between you and God. If I must weep for them yet, though I was the occasion of their deaths and tortures, I cannot much lay it to my account.

"If, by being reputed your leman, as you would have it, I could again set up the Church of God, willingly I would do it. But I see that there is not one man—save maybe some poor simple souls—that would have this done. Each man is set to save his skin and his goods—and you are such a weathercock that I should never blow you to a firm quarter. For what am I set against all this nation?

"If you should say that our wedding was no wedding because of the pre-contract to my cousin Dearham that you have feigned was made—why, I might live as your reputed leman in a secret place. But it is not very certain that even at that I should live very long. For, if I lived, I must work upon you to do the right. And, if that I did, not very long should I live before mine enemies again did come about me and to you. And so I must die. And now I see that you are not such a man as I would live with willingly to preserve my life.

"I speak not to reprove you what I have spoken, but to make you see that as I am so I am. You are as God made you, setting you for His own purposes a weak man in very evil and turbulent times. As a man is born so a man lives; as is his strength so the strain breaks him or he resists the strain. If I have wounded you with these my words, I do ask your pardon. Much of this long speech I have thought upon when I was despondent this long time past. But much of it has come to my lips whilst I spake, and, maybe, it is harsh and rash in the wording. That I would not have, but I may not help myself. I would have you wounded by the things as they are, and by what of conscience you have, in your passions and your prides. And this, I will add, that I die a Queen, but I would rather have died the wife of my cousin Culpepper or of any other simple lout that loved me as he did, without regard, without thought, and without falter. He sold farms to buy me bread. You would not imperil a little alliance with a little King o' Scots to save my life. And this I tell you, that I will spend the last hours of the days that I have to live in considering of this simple man and of his love, and in praying for his soul, for I hear you have slain him! And for the rest, I commend you to your friends!"

The King had staggered back against the long table; his jaw fell open; his head leaned down upon his chest. In all that long speech—the longest she had ever made save when she was shown for Queen—she had not once raised or lowered her voice, nor once dropped her eyes. But she had remembered the lessons of speaking that had been given her by her master Udal, in the aforetime, away in Lincolnshire, where there was an orchard with green boughs, and below it a pig-pound where the hogs grunted.

She went slowly down over the great stone flags of the great hall. It was very gloomy now, and her figure in black velvet was like a small shadow, dark and liquid, amongst shadows that fell softly and like draperies from the roof. Up there it was all dark already, for the light came downwards from the windows. She went slowly, walking as she had been schooled to walk.

"God!" Henry cried out; "you have not played false with Culpepper?" His voice echoed all round the hall.

The Queen's white face and her folded hands showed as she turned—

"Aye, there the shoe pinches!" she said. "Think upon it. Most times you shall not believe it, for you know me. But I have made confession of it before your Council. So it may be true. For I hope some truth cometh to the fore even in Councils."

Near the doorway it was all shadow, and soundlessly she faded away among them. The hinge of the door creaked; through it there came the sound of the pikestaves of her guard upon the stone of the steps. The sound whispered round amidst the statues of old knights and kings that stood upon corbels between the windows. It whispered amongst the invisible carvings of the roof. Then it died away.

The King made no sound. Suddenly he cast his hat upon the paving.

A Note About the Author

Ford Madox Ford (1873–1939) was an English novelist, poet, and editor. Born in Wimbledon, Ford was the son of Pre-Raphaelite artist Catherine Madox Brown and music critic Francis Hueffer. In 1894, he eloped with his girlfriend Elsie Martindale and eventually settled in Winchelsea, where they lived near Henry James and H. G. Wells. Ford left his wife and two daughters in 1909 for writer Isobel Violet Hunt, with whom he launched *The English Review*, an influential magazine that published such writers as Thomas Hardy, Joseph Conrad, Ezra Pound, and D. H. Lawrence. As Ford Madox Hueffer, he established himself with such novels as *The Inheritors* (1901) and *Romance* (1903), cowritten with Joseph Conrad, and *The Fifth Queen* (1906–1907), a trilogy of historical novels. During the Great War, however, he began using the penname Ford Madox Ford to avoid anti-German sentiment. *The Good Soldier* (1915), considered by many to be Ford's masterpiece, earned him a reputation as a leading novelist of his generation and continues to be named among the greatest novels of the twentieth century. Recognized as a pioneering modernist for his poem "Antwerp" (1915) and his tetralogy *Parade's End* (1924–1928), Ford was a friend of James Joyce, Ernest Hemingway, Gertrude Stein, and Jean Rhys. Despite his reputation and influence as an artist and publisher who promoted the early work of some of the greatest English and American writers of his time, Ford has been largely overshadowed by his contemporaries, some of whom took to disparaging him as their own reputations took flight.

A Note from the Publisher

Spanning many genres, from non-fiction essays to literature classics to children's books and lyric poetry, Mint Edition books showcase the master works of our time in a modern new package. The text is freshly typeset, is clean and easy to read, and features a new note about the author in each volume. Many books also include exclusive new introductory material. Every book boasts a striking new cover, which makes it as appropriate for collecting as it is for gift giving. Mint Edition books are only printed when a reader orders them, so natural resources are not wasted. We're proud that our books are never manufactured in excess and exist only in the exact quantity they need to be read and enjoyed.

Discover more of your favorite classics with Bookfinity™.

- Track your reading with custom book lists.
- Get great book recommendations for your personalized Reader Type.
- Add reviews for your favorite books.
- AND MUCH MORE!

Visit **bookfinity.com** and take the fun Reader Type quiz to get started.

Enjoy our classic and modern companion pairings!

Classic & Modern

Printed in the USA
CPSIA information can be obtained
at www.ICGtesting.com
JSHW082342140824
68134JS00020B/1827

9 781513 290812